Behind Whispering

Hands

Linda Ruth Brooks

GUM TREE
press

A copy of this book can be found in the National Library of Australia

Cover Design by Linda Ruth Brooks

ISBN: 978-0-9808161-4-3
Fiction/Contemporary women

Behind Whispering Hands is a work of fiction. Any similarity
between the characters in this book and real people, living or dead, is
coincidental.

This book, and others by Linda Ruth Brooks, can be found at
www.amazon.com, online bookstores and other retail outlets.

Behind whispering hands
lie seeds of suspicion
nurtured through the soil
of discontent
and spread
like midnight shrouds
unchecked

Behind whispering hands
in the womb
sheltered from the world
words begin in secret flutterings
draw tentative breath
and become
other

Behind whispering hands
lies become fact
twisting and turning
reaching beyond truth
grow, then fly
travel undeterred
afar

Ellie

Ellie strained towards the gate in the evening air as it if would bring her closer to Duncan. He was hardly ever late, but tonight he was—and by half an hour. That half an hour was precious time. Of course it hadn't been in the beginning. Duncan had had to work hard to gain a moment of her attention in the early days.

Ellie threw her cigarette on the ground and crushed it angrily. She would not be treated like this. Slipping her clutch firmly under her arm she turned on her heel. Waiting in the laneway beside the house wasn't her idea of sophistication, but knocking on the front door was out of the question. Her parents would never approve of their sixteen year old daughter roaming all over town on the back of a motorcycle with a mechanic. Image was everything for the Belmores.

1

Then she heard it—the sound of the Harley. He was coming. Her heart quickened. A smile lit up her face—a smile she quickly schooled into a nonchalant expression.

The engine purred to a standstill. In one deft movement he slipped his helmet off. Ellie regarded him through slanted eyes, standing back, arms folded.

'You're late, Duncan Antona.'

'Oh come on, Babe. I can't leave when I like. I'm not free until the job's done. You know that. I'm a working class man.'

'So you keep telling me.'

'Some of us have to clock in and out, you know. Anyway, that's why you love me. I'm a real man.' Duncan's arm snaked out to enclose her. 'Not like those "suits" you're used to through the modelling agency.'

Ellie gave him a punishing kiss, intense and sweet then withdrew, leaving cool air to fill the space between.

'Tease,' he said, 'I'll pay you back for that.'

Ellie shivered in anticipation.

All the guys in her social circle would have begged forgiveness and promised the world. Not Duncan. He sat astride the bike and waited.

'So do I get to meet your parents? Is that your house, the two storey mansion?'

Ellie pouted.

'Oh, I see. You're keeping me at arm's length because you're worried about me being after your wealth, fame and beauty.'

Ellie let out a relieved sigh. Her secret was safe, for now. 'Well, are you?' she asked, smiling.

'Beauty maybe, but you can keep the rest.' There was a bitter edge to his voice.

'Oh?'

'Yeah, people with shedloads of money don't care about anyone but themselves. So, gorgeous, I'm making a big exception with you.' Duncan slipped his coat off. 'Well, if you're going to stand back there at least take my coat to keep the chill out.

Ellie moved closer to take the coat and Duncan's arm snaked out and pulled her to him. She squealed and surrendered to his lips.

'And I thought you just wanted a model girlfriend.' Ellie deepened the kiss.

'Nah. I picked you out of the crowd because you're different from the other models. I don't know how, you're just sweeter, natural. Honestly, I don't think much of your friends. Bit too skinny and coked up for my liking.'

'Well, I'm not actually...' she began, but Duncan swung one leg over the bike, drew her close and kissed her into silence.

She would tell him later that she was only the receptionist. He wouldn't care. It was exhilarating. He hadn't singled her out because he wanted a model, a perfect woman. He'd wanted *her*, Ellie. If she could outshine the gorgeous Tatum with her copper waist length hair and endless legs and all the other girls, she must really be worth something.

'Not that I'm complaining about the packaging,' he said, beginning a slow exploration of her breasts, 'or those long legs' he slipped a caressing hand along her thigh.

She drew in a ragged breath.

'Later, sweetheart.' Duncan held her arms firmly and set her back a step. She whimpered at the distance.

He slowly purred the motor and glided to the end of the road, then turning into the roundabout he gunned the engine with a delighted laugh. Ellie slapped his muscled arm. If her parents found out there'd be hell to pay.

Ellie realised just how much she wanted this, wanted Duncan. It had ceased to be a game, a rich girl's rebellion. He'd used the word love tonight. Winding her arms around him she whispered 'I love you' into his neck. It was a daring act. A thrill zapped as she said the words. Then filled with doubt she hoped he hadn't heard.

'Thanks Babe.' Duncan accelerated the bike and leaned back, holding the front tyre in the air and let out a yell of primal satisfaction.

Ellie sighed. He loved her. She hoped the night would never end.

James Belmore was waiting for his daughter when she tiptoed barefoot in the door at 4:30 am. He still wore the suit he had on the day before.

Ellie raised a trembling hand to her dishevelled hair. A bra strap hung from her handbag, hastily placed there hours before. Her attempts to hide its presence only increased the cold fury of her father. He was seldom angry, but when he was, his anger was all the more powerful for his cool, unflinching demeanour.

'Who have you been with Ellie?' His soft query startled her.

Ellie flustered. Her father always caught her off guard. Her mother would have asked where she'd been and that would have been a far easier question, giving her time to cover her nerves and keep her cool.

'Well...I...he...'

'Who?' The one word was a shard of ice in the room. 'I've got all the time in the world, Ellie. You will tell me who the boy is. I heard a motorcycle. A Harley if I'm not mistaken.'

Ellie hiccupped and cried her way through the whole tale, feeling tainted in the telling. 'I'm sorry, Daddy. He's not like the other downtown boys. He has a job. He lives clean,' she

sniffed, then raised her head. It was a step towards defiance.
'Anyway...I hate the snobbery of our lives.'

Her father's eyes flared. She held herself stiff.

'I am the son of a tool maker, Ellie. Don't give me that elitist crap you and your friends bandy about. We've never forbidden you to see anyone—unless they're criminals. Is he a criminal, Ellie?'

Her father's tone finished the last of her pride.

'No, Daddy.' Ellie looked down, her voice weak.

'Then, he's good enough to walk into my house. Why didn't he walk into my house, Ellie? Hmm?'

'Well, I thought...well, he wanted to...but I told him not to, you know how Mum is.'

'Don't use your mother.' Her father's fury was white hot now. He took in her messy hair and unnatural glow and prayed his suspicions were wrong. But, panther-like, he took his time.

'You told him not to—that's it?'

'Yes, it's not his fault. You have to understand that.'

'*Do I?* How old is he?'

'Twenty.'

'And just how old does he think you are?'

'The same,' she murmured, head down.

'Why would he think that?'

'I...well ...'

'You lied about your age.' James Belmore paused. 'He thinks he's dating a woman, not a sixteen year old school drop out.'

Ellie's flushed. Her father's summation stung.

But he wasn't finished. He delivered the next words with focused deliberation. 'How far?'

'Wha...' Ellie faltered, hating his concise manner.

'You know what I mean, girl.'

Ellie flushed bright red and lowered her eyes.

Her father was silent, hard eyes on his eldest daughter.

'So, that's how it is. Right. Now, here is how it will be. You will not see this boy again. Do you understand me? If you are pregnant you will work out a solution *with him*, and if you are not, and you had better pray you aren't, then you may stay here and prove yourself. You will leave that trumped-up job at the modelling agency and undertake some course. Considering your school results—perhaps some reception course at the local TAFE.'

Ellie made one last attempt and blustered, 'I just wanted to save him from standing up to you.'

It was a mistake.

'Ellie, how little you know—about life, and yourself. A real man will have to stand up to *you*.'

As he turned to walk out the door Ellie thought she heard him say 'too much like your mother'.

Ellie was in agony. Her blasted father. If he had ranted and raved she would have made a defiant exit and hurled him a stinging tirade. That always worked with her mother. But, typical of him, he'd left her hanging. Left her with all the questions she had avoided the past idyllic months. Pregnant. Would Duncan welcome her with open arms with a baby on the way? How would they survive—he lived over a garage, doubling as security.

She spent the night writhing, alone with her thoughts. Mum would have given her a sleeping pill, but that meant the risk of fronting her father, and she was not speaking to him again, ever.

The bleep of her mobile shocked her awake at noon. It was Duncan. She shut the drawer. She'd read it later.

Later was a long time coming.

Ellie was lost. The thrill had paled. Life had gone flat with crushing speed. She did love Duncan, she did. She just didn't know what to say. Not yet. But she couldn't leave it too long. Or could she? This could be the way out. But she didn't want out. Damn, she didn't know what she wanted. She had the whole weekend ahead of her, but no one to turn to. Tatum and the models wouldn't want to hear her teen angst. She wasn't really part of the group. She'd been pretending.

If Ellie thought her father's calm would be annoying she

hadn't counted on her mother, Angie, taking her frigid indifference to a whole new level. She was angry. Then she plummeted into the anxiety of an unplanned pregnancy and every other worry paled in comparison.

Work kept her busy and she was breezy and busy when her friends texted or she ran into them when she was out. Her father had meant business about the job at the modelling agency. He'd already phoned Sylvia, her boss.

'So lovely for you to go to Tafe, Ellie,' Sylvia had said, with her usual calm poise. 'A nice little career for you. You can stay on here until Tafe begins, love. That will help you save for textbooks and things.'

Ellie had paled. Her father hadn't even allowed her the dignity of resigning. She was wretched. Any buying her own textbooks? Dad really had blabbered. Ellie was suddenly glad she was leaving. It was hell having a boss who was your mother's best friend and in your father's pocket.

'Thanks Sylvia,' she muttered.

'Your seventeen soon, aren't you. Your mother will plan a wonderful party.'

'Not this year,' Ellie spat. She gave Sylvia a malignant stare. Of course the woman knew her father had vetoed a party. He might as well have vetoed her whole life.

Ellie's periods were late which only added to her wretchedness. She reluctantly sent Duncan ambiguous texts in answer to his—adding xxxs. She hadn't answered his phone calls. It was too hard. Her nervous stumbling to the toilet to check if her period had arrived was bound to be interrupted by one or other of her three siblings.

At least Robert, who was four years older, wouldn't be a problem—he was hardly ever home, and if he was, he always used his own ensuite bathroom upstairs. But just to be safe, if she heard the soft footfall of Robert's expensive shoes—she waited. Long years had taught her the difference between his gait and his father's. If she heard Sara's clattering high heels—*and who didn't*—she waited. If she heard Lucy with her bare feet or whatever crazy footwear she was currently favouring—she waited. Because even though Lucy was tiny and cheerful, she was the most fearsome of them all with her straightforward I-don't-care attitude.

Ellie moaned. They had five bathrooms for goodness sake—why had everyone suddenly decided it was too far to go to the upstairs bathrooms? She wasn't going up there when her father was in his office pretending to work. Did her sisters have to make her a spectacle? They couldn't possible know. Oh, who was she kidding, everyone in the family knew everything that went on in this house. With the possible exception of Robert, who didn't give a damn, bless him.

She would have to ask for an upstairs bedroom. When

she was back in favour, of course. Which could take *forever*.

When her period finally arrived early one Wednesday morning Ellie shrieked. Angie dropped a crystal vase. James took a headache pill. Sara banged on the door to ask if she was all right—and if she was, could she please make a move as there were other people to think about.

Oh, who cared—she wasn't pregnant. She'd survived the worst month of her life.

She was never having sex again.

Lucy

Lucy paused at the doorway to the garage, suddenly unsure of herself. Everyone in the family would say she was meddling. She smiled. When had that stopped her before?

The man working on the car was impressive. She expected a weedy, sneering rebel, but Duncan Antona looked as wholesome as a guy from a shaving ad.

He turned towards her and smiled as he wiped his hands on a rag.

'Whatcha doing kid? You're not allowed in here, y'know. OH&S. Occupational Health...'

'...and Safety, I know,' said Lucy. 'Will you get into trouble with the boss—having a 'kid' in here?'

Duncan merely pointed a greasy spanner at a sign over the office door—D ANTONA, AUTOMOTIVE

ELECTRICIAN. 'Didn't you read the sign on the building on the way in? I'm the boss—such as it is. Duncan Antona. Are you lost?' He picked up a rag and wiped the grease off his hands.

'No.'

'Why are you here?'

'I'm Ellie Belmore's sister. Lucy. I just...well, felt bad. Dad found out, about you, and she's dumping you, but she won't tell you. She never does...not that she's mean...um...she just...Oh, I don't know why I came. I just thought you deserved...you know, an explanation.'

Lucy blushed. That hadn't been quite her intention, but finding Duncan looking so, well normal, distracted her.

'How old are you, kid?' Duncan watched her perch onto a tall stool just inside the door.

'I'm fourteen. Mum had three of us girls one after the other, fourteen, fift...' Lucy paled and hesitated. She hadn't intended to give Ellie's age away.

'So Little Miss Fix-It, you thought you'd put me out of my misery? Do you always go around trying to sort things out for people?'

'Oh yes, Mum says I'm a terrible trial. She won't let me see my Nan anymore because she says I talk too much to her and tire her out, but I know it's because she's scared Nan might say something she doesn't want me to hear.'

Duncan's brow furrowed.

'My nan has dementia, but she's fine most of the time. She upsets the family by saying 'It will all end in tears'. Goodness knows what that means...I miss her. I'll visit her when I get a car.' Duncan's eyebrows shot up and Lucy's voice faltered. 'Um...I'm sorry, I talk too much.'

'That's okay. Gets pretty quiet in here.'

'Sounded pretty noisy to me on the way in.'

Duncan laughed. What a cute kid—so open. But he couldn't have her hanging around.

'That all you wanted to tell me?'

'Well, yeah. I just thought you'd want to know she wouldn't be calling. So, you know—you could get over her and stuff.'

'Is the rest of the family like you?'

'Oh no. I'm the odd one out. I say all the wrong things at the wrong time. Which doesn't make sense to me because it can't be both, y'know? It's either the wrong thing altogether or the right thing at the wrong time.'

'Seems you've got it all squared up, kid.'

Lucy scrambled down off the stool, trying to hold her long, flowery dress, her hat and backpack. The hat fell off and Duncan picked it up.

'...er...nice hat, kid. Seems a bit...ah...big for you though,' he said.

15

'Oh. Yes. My Aunt Clare gave it to me. She's the arty one in the family. Designs stuff out of broken plates and old things. She makes these really funky hats—this isn't one of them—her designs are...way-out colours and materials—you know felt and bits...'

'She doesn't sound like the rest of the family.'

'I guess not. Mum says we have to be polite and tolerate her, but I think she's cool.'

Duncan clenched his teeth. 'Ah, not up to the family standard hey?'

Lucy frowned. 'I don't know how to tell you, but Ellie's just turned seventeen, she was only...'

'Shit!' Duncan paled. 'Sixteen.'

'Oh dear.'

'Sorry kid.' He handed her the hat. 'Look, thanks. I'm okay.'

She flipped it on, adjusting it by the brim by looking at the ribbon hanging over the edge. It was an awkward motion and pulled her fine curls over her face. She shrugged the backpack in place and then swiped her hair to the side in order to see. Duncan tried not to laugh.

Lucy turned serious eyes to him.

'You won't tell Ellie, will you? I mean...about me coming. She says I have foot and mouth disease as it is.'

Duncan zipped his fingers over his lips and watched her

climb onto the bike and ride away. He watched her brace forward and pedal like the wind down the street.

Lucy Belmore was trouble all right. He wouldn't want to maintain any car she drove when she grew up, and God only knows how she would fare with her transparent honesty in the brutal social world of adults.

'Hey, Luce! Look out! You nearly ran me down!'

'Well, what are you doing in my way Jason?'

'Well, Jeez Luce, I might be standing right where you told me to wait—to bring my bike back. I'm your partner in crime—remember?'

'Well, don't call me Luce. You make me sound like a pack of potatoes...or worse—the way our family is going.' She paused, sighed and gave him a shy smile. 'I'm sorry Jason, but I feel such an idiot. What was I thinking? Going to visit my sister's...well...who knows what? A complete stranger.'

'Oh Luc*eee*. You weren't thinking, that's what.'

'I know. I'm too impulsive. I feel so embarrassed. Riding a boy's bike—*that I'm not used to,* wobbling around like I need L plates, wearing a hat instead of a...'

'Well, I did try with the helmet, Lucy...'

'I know. I just didn't want to look like a kid, but he called me one anyway.'

'Well, you do look eleven going on twelve...ouch, what d'ya do that for? Don't take it out on me just because you decided to act like an adult when you should still be on formula. Well, what did he say about Ellie?'

Lucy scratched her head. 'Nothing.'

'Well, what did you talk about?'

'Hmm, you know—I don't remember exactly.'

'Would that be because you rattled on and didn't give the guy a chance to get a word in sideways? Actually that probably worked for him come to think of it. Men hate talking about that kind of stuff. Especially with a 'kid'. I told you it was a stupid idea.'

Lucy handed Jason the bike. 'I know. Mum's right, I'm a meddler.'

'I was worried. You took so long. What if the guy had been a beer swilling drunk, or a druggie, or someone who ravaged girls?'

'That's why I brought you.'

'Yeah, right.' Jason laughed and held up a puny arm.

Later, sitting at her desk attempting to start her homework, Lucy gave herself a stern lecture. No more meddling.

Lucy was shocked at Ellie's behaviour. Risking pregnancy. Lying about her age to someone she spouted that she loved, and then lying to their parents. She would have to know she'd be found out.

It was all the fault of those flaky girls at work with their expensive makeup that looked like cement in the daylight.

Giving herself a shake, she banged the text book on her head and prepared to get stuck into it. Damn. Where were her glasses? Dad would kill her if she lost them again. Straining her overwrought brain brought a sinking feeling as she remembered sliding them into her pocket after school. The pocket with the hole. They could be anywhere.

She opened the textbook but it was no good, she couldn't read a word. She couldn't borrow a pair to get by. There were none in the house. Why was everyone in her family so frigging perfect with their 20/20 vision? Even Dad, who was positively ancient, didn't need them. Blast.

Without her glasses, Lucy was left to daydream. Her talk with Duncan had triggered thoughts of Aunt Clare. She had a wicked sense of humour and the girls loved having her to visit. Sometimes her eyes were sad, but that didn't last long. Mum never seemed to be pleased with her, but then Lucy couldn't think of anyone who came up to her mother's exacting standards.

She giggled when she thought of Margaret, the housekeeper, and her early days with the family. She was a brilliant cook, but Mum made her so nervous that Dad had to ban Mum from the kitchen so 'they didn't all starve'.

Clare left the farm in Tenterfield to live at Leura in the Blue Mountains when Lucy was only two, so her memories of the farm didn't include Clare. Lucy loved the farm, but Gramps died when she was eight, and the family left and moved to Vaucluse, with Nan having a unit nearby. Then their visits to Leura stopped.

'It's too far to travel to Clare's cottage,' Mum said, 'and it's really too small for our crowd.'

So Clare came to them, staying at Nan's flat. Any meals together were at restaurants—'to make things easier'.

Lucy chewed the end of pen. She felt silly being vague about Clare when she'd mentioned her to Duncan. They hardly ever spoke of Clare at home.

Truth be told, she felt silly about the whole visit to Duncan. She'd been as clear as mud about her reasons for going there. Now she was glad. Ellie could sort out her own life.

But the conversation with Duncan about Clare had set her mind on a path, and typical of Lucy, she didn't want to let go. She tried to remember Clare's cottage. She was struck with the thought that she could only remember seeing Clare's home in photographs that were relegated to the bottom of the living room drawers. She missed Clare.

The family were driving her mad. Why couldn't she visit Clare? She travelled nearly that distance to school every day.

'Why are you always in the way, Ellie? You're going to the

loo more times than Nan, and she has incontinence pads!'
yelled Sara, her voice echoing upstairs.

Lucy moaned. Sisters—who'd have them? Obviously Sara
had missed the whole 'pregnancy scare'. So like Sara. She
certainly was the family dreamer. She never fought with
anyone so Ellie must really be raising hell. At least her
periods had arrived. There'd been quite a hullaballoo about
that, even though their parents and Ellie tried to 'keep the
noise down, for goodness sake'.

That was months ago. Now the fight over the bathroom
was because Ellie was trying to accustom herself to
'outrageous hours' and getting ready at the same time as
Sara. She was doing some fancy PA course, having barely
escaped having to study with 'peasants'.

'Shut up, Sara. You're so loud in the mornings. I can't be
late.'

'Welcome to the world of working class schleps, Ellie.
The real world awaits your Royal Highness.'

Lucy sighed and thanked the gods of zipped lips that she
hadn't mentioned anything about the pregnancy drama to
Duncan. She'd intended to, but was deeply grateful she'd
kept her mouth shut on that score. Not that it was due to
self-control, but to the shock of Duncan looking like the boy
next door and having the nicest manners, *like ever*. Boys her
age were awkward and blunt, even Jason. And what was the

point of telling him anything when the 'scare' was over. He need never know.

Ellie was screaming back at Sara—something about moving upstairs. Oh no! Life wouldn't be worth living with Ellie down the hall. All of this made a visit to Clare more attractive, well, necessary, when you came right down to it.

Lucy began rehearsing speeches to her parents, desperately trying to find an angle that would appeal to their personal gain.

Parents were like that.

James

There was no way around it—his decision to have a home office was one of the worst ideas ever. Sitting in his upstairs office, James Belmore tried to concentrate on the fax that had just arrived.

It was no use. He put the sheet of paper aside, hoping he'd find it later. Now, if he had a secretary here—but that had been one of the inevitable losses of relocating his office. There was no one to keep a check on his paperwork. He hadn't realised how important his secretary was to his organisational ability. In short, without her, he had none.

The clatter going on downstairs was beyond annoying. Ellie was still the demanding diva she'd always been. Her humility had only lasted a few weeks. She was yelling at Sara. 'Move it will you—some of us have real work. I would appreciate a *little* understanding—if that's possible from the barbarians in this house.'

'James,' said Angie, poking her head in the door. 'Would you like a pot of tea? I've been neglecting you, but the room looks wonderful. The caterers have taken over, so why don't you and I have a few moments before the rush and bustle.'

'What's tonight about? I've forgotten.'

'Honestly James, it's just a small dinner party. Sylvia, some of the girls and Robert and his lot.'

'Sara and Ellie are at it again. They're making enough noise for a construction crew. Where's Lucy?'

'Studying with Jason. I can't believe she's the only one being quiet.'

'She might surprise us and be the least of our worries,' said James.

'We can dream,' laughed Angie. She worried her lip with her bottom teeth.

'What is it, Ange? I know that look. Something on your mind?'

'It's Robert. He seemed to be ready to make a commitment to Rachel, but now Tatum, that empty-headed model friend of Ellie's seems to be moving in on him. Not what I'd want for him.'

'That half-dressed redhead?'

'James, really.' Angie gave his arm a slap. 'Typical man— that's all you notice.'

'Bit hard to ignore. It's going to be quite a houseful when they all get married. It will be more than four then. That will be a shock we hadn't counted on, especially as we were only having two...' James began.

'Is all that fuss in the dining room for only two people? I thought Dad had a business dinner.' It was Sara, poking her head in the door. 'You'd better come down, Mum. The caterers are arguing over the centrepiece. I told them I was the upstairs maid.'

'Oh Sara, you didn't!'

'Don't worry, Mum. I didn't curtsy.'

'Honestly, Sara, you're getting as bad as Lucy.'

'Ooh, do you think so? How marvellous.'

Angie swiped at Sara as they both left for downstairs.

James slumped in the chair. Angie gave all the appearance of sailing serenely through troubled waters, but if he knew Angie she was well stocked up on sedatives. Thank goodness she didn't take them often. He didn't blame her for resorting to the small bottle in her bedside table. In the past weeks he'd been tempted to ask her for one. He couldn't be as blasé as Angie about the pregnancy scare and Ellie's lies. Sixteen was much too young for that drama. What lay ahead with the girl? He hasn't asked Angie for a pill, he'd had a whisky then punched the pillow into submission and turned to stare into the night sky.

He would have liked to punch that young hooligan who had been secretly courting his daughter, but after Ellie's attitude he couldn't raise his ire for the young man. Ellie was doing enough deceiving for the pair of them. And anyway, there was every sign that the romance was over. After all, the young bloke had been deceived too, and probably not just by her age.

They shouldn't have let Ellie leave school and work for the modelling agency. Hanging out with the older, streetwise girls had given her ideas. Most of her model friends had travelled the world, thought nothing of meeting celebrities or 'medicinally enhancing their performance'. Sylvia had promised to keep an eye on things, but a lot of help that had been. At least Ellie seemed to be enjoying the office management course. There was no more mention of Duncan Antona. But would Ellie stay out of trouble.

Another thing bothered him. The boy's name was familiar. James remembered his father, Darius Antona, as a brilliant mechanic who had died quite suddenly from a malignant melanoma. James' company had often used the Antonas' mechanical services. Darius left four sons if James remembered it right, raising the boys alone after his wife died at least a decade ago. He'd been planning the oldest son's wedding when he was diagnosed.

James wondered how things had fared for the four boys.

Probably taking care of one another—the Antonas upheld a strong sense of family. He envied Mediterranean families their way of life. Even though the wife was Australian, there were strong extended family ties.

He thought one or two of them worked in the family business. He might just ask around. Wouldn't hurt. He chuckled. Women weren't the only ones with an 'information network'. His curiosity was piqued. It would be interesting to see what had become of the family.

A twinge of guilt speared him. He didn't even know if his company was still using their services, or if the place was still viable. He'd have to check with his secretary. It would certainly be bad form if the company had just dumped them without so much as a sympathy message.

But all this introspection was getting him nowhere. He eyed the whiskey decanter. Hmm. It seemed lower. He picked it up. Yes, definitely less. Robert was hardly ever around, and didn't like the stuff. Lucy and Sara were off the list, and Ellie had taken a liking to those fruity spritzer things. Damn.

Mark

'For God's sake Bert, stop fussing like an old woman and help me out.' Mark Henderson ground out the words. He stared out of the smeared window of the dull fish and chip shop. He turned his head. Was that Julia Penshurst of the Tenterfield Tribune? A quick glance gave him the relief that it wasn't the reporter. He was becoming paranoid.

'Don't get me wrong, Mark. I'd do anything for you, but you're asking me to break the law.' Bert sighed and wished he wasn't in the Mayor's debt.

'Well, passing the additional space on your planning application wasn't exactly above board. I did that for our friendship.'

'And ten thousand dollars,' said Bert.

'That was a campaign donation. Don't insult me, Bert. I'm not about money, you know that.'

'I'd be risking my business. I've been a pharmacist all my life. I'm getting close to retirement, Mark. You should be thinking about the same.'

'I'll be on the job while ever the voters want me, Bert. There's a lot this town needs. Don't change the subject. Just get me the painkillers. The same one's Millie takes. Surely you can pass them off as my wife's.'

'It's not that easy. They're S4s. You should have a prescription.'

'Don't give me jargon. You're messing me around. Can't you see I'm in agony?'

'Why don't you see a doctor?' asked Bert.

'I told you. I can't have any rumours right now. Council is pushing to get the development through for Jim Crenshaw.'

Bert snorted. 'The one you went on the record to say you'd stop?'

'I'm not here to talk politics. I get enough of that everywhere else.'

'You have to at least tell me what symptoms you have. It's on my conscience, Mark. What happened?'

'The council meeting went late. I stopped on the way home to take a leak. You know what that's like at our age...Well, this young kid came out of nowhere and kicked me...you know where.'

'Why don't you tell the police? Jeez, Mark, that's a crime!'

Mark buckled over, too tired to argue. He sighed. 'Look, the kid is the son of a friend. He thought I was a prowler. It was dark. He freaked out to have some old bloke peeing on a tree. Look, it's just a misunderstanding, but if I don't have something for pain, I'll go insane.'

'This was last night?'

'Yes. I took two of Millie's pills to get some sleep, but I'm going to be wretched for days yet. I can't keep taking hers, she need them. Happy now, Detective Mason?'

'Must have been quite a whack. Okay, look, I can get you one bottle, but you have to promise that you'll see a doctor if it doesn't get better.'

'All right Dr Freaking Oz. I promise. Do you want me to 'pinky swear' as well?'

'Very funny. Come on then, the things I do for my friends,' said Bert, slapping Mark on the back as he led him to the back door of the pharmacy.

'Arr!' Mark flinched, then swore.

'Get sunburnt too, mate?' Bert laughed.

'You try hitting a barbed wire fence on the way down to the ground.'

Bert chuckled. 'Damn shame I can't tell anyone this. It's a classic.'

'You do and I'll have you hung, drawn and quartered.

That's a promise,' said Mark.

'Jeez, all right. You don't have to get your knickers in a twist.' Bert roared laughing at his own joke. Mark was silent. 'You sounded like you meant that, Mr Mayor.'

You better believe it, thought Mark Henderson.

On his way home in the car, Mark chewed three of the tablets. He wasn't waiting for water. Or something stronger to get the pills down. Soon he would feel the pain ebb away. Then he could relax. And forget.

Forget that he'd been kicked in the groin by a huge bear of a man with steel-capped boots. Forget that he'd been taking his pleasure with little Katie Morris, the office work experience girl. Forget her screams and her shock, her clawing and bucking to escape. Forget that he had no idea if the man who'd interrupted that act had recognised him. Forget that his back was torn by Katie's fingernails, taking his DNA with her. Forget about the others: all young, fresh and admiring—wanting to learn from the 'great man'. Forget about living a lie to Millie and his four daughters.

But most of all, forget that his father had come home from the war and been drunk every night. Forget that his mother had been beaten into defeated silence and stopped trying to protect her son. Forget how much he hated them both.

He might show up on Anzac and Remembrance Day, lay wreaths and praise his father, delivering fine speeches on Jack Henderson's status as a war hero, and eulogise his time as a POW in a Japanese camp in Western Thailand. He might put his hand on his heart, and murmur *Lest We Forget* with the crowd—but all the while he was thinking, 'If only I could'.

Linda Brooks

Sara

Sara had a simple philosophy about her family. If her parents were worrying over her sisters, they weren't bothering her. And if she feigned ignorance about what went on in the house, her life was easier.

It was over four years since Ellie's scandalous affair, but Sara knew the memory of it lingered in their minds—Mum was downstairs outdoing herself for Ellie's 21st Birthday party. Ellie had moaned about having a party for her 21st, until she realised it would be a wonderful opportunity to show the delicious Brian Denton off to her friends. Sara wouldn't be surprised if Ellie was hoping it would be a good time to receive a proposal.

It was certainly something Mum was hoping for. Getting Ellie married off would be a coup, but more than that, a relief. She always seemed to be one step away from disaster.

Ellie's voice carried up the stairs. 'Don't go overboard, Mum! I don't want a dinner party. I told you I wanted a smorgasbord in the garden.'

'We have family as well as your guests to think about Ellie.' Angie's voice was worn.

'Who, Mother? Nana and Aunt Clare won't be here. Even Lucy has taken herself off to visit Clare. Which I must say is a relief, she's a walking social disaster.'

Sara was offended for Lucy, but she wasn't going to stick her neck into the argument downstairs.

It wasn't that Lucy really had 'disasters', it was more that she made every life event a potential drama. Even the simplest conversation could take serious turns when Lucy was in the mix. Which was precisely why Sara loved her so much. Darling Lucy, life would be so dull without her. Anyway, the better part of Lucy's supposed trouble was due to her alarming propensity to tell the truth. This would have been a bonus in many homes, but not theirs.

The fact that Lucy sometimes misread situations only made for more drama in the family, and panic by their mother in particular. All of which was enormously entertaining. Sara wished she had half Lucy's talent. If there was anyone on God's green earth who deserved to be disconcerted, it was their mother, Angie.

Sara worried that it was unnatural to feel this way about

her mother, but not enough to bother about it. She felt sorry for Lucy—bumbling through life with the best of intentions to please both their parents—without the slightest hope of success. It was no good even trying to tell her. It went over her head. Anyway, Sara was limited by what she could say to advice Lucy, because of the very fact that she was pretending *not* to know anything. Which was at least less than the facade of the others in a family where pretence was a way of life.

Sara heard a loud snoring sound. She almost jumped out of her chair to go downstairs, but then she remembered their mother had a habit of falling asleep in the early afternoon. It was her sherry time, but Sara "didn't know" about that either.

Reaching into her desk drawer, she retrieved Lucy's glasses. Even though they'd been missing for four years, Sara knew they'd been expensive and Lucy had copped a scalding lecture from both parents and make to wear an old ugly pair. She hated Lucy getting into trouble. It wasn't as if she'd held on to the glasses for that long, anyway. She'd wanted Lucy to have them, but it would be difficult to explain how she came to have them, so she decided to put them somewhere obvious, and say nothing. It would never do to lie. In her experience that was hardly ever necessary. She glided down and slipped the glasses behind the silverware cabinet. The cleaning lady would find them there at the end of the week.

Back up in her room she sorted through her desk drawers, pulled out the page in the newspaper that advertised for a job with an art company. Flicking on her laptop she soon became engrossed in researching the company and writing her résumé. She wanted this part-time job badly. With only a year and a half to go she should have a chance at the job. Her art studies were going really well at Uni. She'd recently won second prize in a state wide exhibition.

'Really, Sara. I thought better of you.' It was Lucy—dangling her glasses.

Sara had to grab the desk to avoid falling off the chair.

'Jeez, Lucy! You scared the life out of me.'

'And well I should.'

'I can explain.'

'This should be good,' said Lucy, leaning on the door jamb. 'Are you a coward by choice? Or was it thrust upon you? I saw you Sara! Dropping the glasses where only the maid would find them.'

'Wha...I've got a good reason. Anyway I don't...I hate confrontation. It would have been all right if you hadn't seen me put them there?'

'Oh really?'

'I didn't want to upset you. I can't talk to you when you're like this.' A tear formed in the corner of Sara's eye, and although she fought, it trickled down her cheek. 'I'm sorry, Sis. I didn't know what to say. I didn't want to hurt you, really. I only just found them,' she said, 'at Duncan's.'

'You didn't think I knew that you were visiting Duncan?' Sara's mouth formed an 0, and she froze.

Lucy sat down. 'How long have you had my glasses? That's what I want to know?'

'Oh, only a few weeks, honestly.'

'But I lost them over four years ago.'

'I know. Duncan didn't see them. You know what men are like. He felt bad. He said you'd been asking about them. He nearly fainted when I told him they were worth $1500 and his brother had just left them in a grubby tool box in the back room. He works there tidying up...'

'...redistributing the mess,' said Lucy, smiling. 'I know, I go there too—you know.'

They both giggled. Duncan teased his younger brother no end, but liked having him around. Now Lucy and Sara realised they shared a knowledge of Duncan. The girls eyed each other warily.

'So, how did ...' began Sara.

'About that explanation...'

'Oh. That. One of the guys in my jewellery making class...'

'The one you take in the evenings?'

'Yes. Jeez Lucy, you really do know everything.'

Lucy gave a dismissive wave.

'Well, he said he knew a guy with a back room where we could hang out and practice. Duncan's father used to do fine work when he wasn't fixing cars, so there were lots of great tools there, thin nose pliers and...'

'Oh, do spare me the boring bits.'

'Well, we rummaged through one of the boxes and there were your glasses.'

'That's it?'

Sara shrugged.

'You're kidding me! You went through all that angst in your head, hid my glasses—rather than hand them to me and tell the blooming truth. The good old simple truth.'

'The truth isn't always that simple.'

'Yes, it is. *Telling* the truth—*that's* the complicated part.'

'Don't take the high moral ground with me. You're not perfect. You get into enough trouble for three people.'

Lucy glared. Sara cowered.

'I take my stripes when I stuff up, Sara. Don't get high and mighty. Ellie does that enough for all of us,' Lucy said. 'So what do you think of Duncan?'

'He's all right, I guess. Okay! Minor crush going on. But he was with Ellie back then. I don't want to get hurt, you know.'

'From my *limited* experience,' said Lucy, 'getting hurt is

part of life, and hiding under a rock doesn't exclude that from happening.'

'When did you get so wise? I'm impressed.'

'Yesterday. Now, show me those papers.' Lucy made a grab and Sara struggled with them half-heartedly. Both girls were giggling.

'Come on, I'm your sister—who else can you confide in?' said Lucy. 'Mind you, I have to be out of here in a few minutes.' She pointed to her packed suitcase. 'Jason is taking me to the train to Clare's. Do enjoy the party for me, won't you?'

Sara poked her tongue out.

'Oh, and in case you're interested,' added Lucy, peeking around the door. 'Duncan never stops talking about you.'

'Really? Does he?'

'Aha! You lurve him!' Lucy squealed with delight.

'*Lucy!*'

'What?'

Sara threw a pillow at her, but it was too late. Lucy was bounding down the stairs. She smiled, she should have trusted Lucy. It was good to feel close to her again. Lucy had been spending a lot of time with their aunt Clare. Maybe it was time to go with her. She remembered her last visit.

Some of the details were vague. It had been bitterly cold. There was only her, Mum and Clare. She'd been told to stay outside and play. She had really been looking forward to a nice visit. There had been many visits to Clare's cottage when the family lived back in Tenterfield. All four kids ran wild and free, chatting to neighbours over the old paling fence and hiding in the corrugated iron sheds. But that day in Leura was different.

Sara played hopscotch by herself. Jumping on the lovely stones imbedded in the ground. There was a gate to the back yard. Peeping over it offered a view of colour and lush foliage. If she jumped she could see a beautiful sun dial. She saw a birdbath—ancient and mossy, where the birds frolicked even in the chilly waters. She'd walked along the crooked stone wall on her tip toes. Then she huddled near the door. Her mother's voice was raised.

'It's no good, Clare. It's too much to expect...' Their voices faded.

Sara shivered. Why hadn't Robert or the others come along for the visit? At least Lucy. Where was Dad? It was so cold. Pulling the sheepskin collar of her coat up around her neck, Sara curled into a ball and slipped into dreamless sleep.

Things changed after that, not just with Clare, but at home.

Angie

Bent over the oak table Angie hummed as she polished it. When it glistened she added the lace tablecloth and placed the floral centrepiece. She really wanted Ellie's 21st birthday party to go well. Standing back with satisfaction she rubbed the gnawing ache in her lower back.

Never mind, she could leave things to the staff now. She wanted to be rested for Ellie's sake. After all, that's what tonight was all about. She had been dating the lovely young Denton boy for two years now.

Thank God, Ellie was over that nonsense with the biker boy. That had given her more grey hairs than she cared to count. But the girl had seen sense, and even though James hadn't agreed with her, Angie was sure the new wardrobe and makeover helped turn things around. Men never understood the power of a new look to get a new attitude.

Tall, and thin as a reed, Angie Belmore had done her day's work. The planning and supervision for tonight's party had exhausted her. She looked at her diamond filigree watch, the one James had bought her in Paris. It was 2pm. The caterers would arrive in an hour. Just enough time to phone her mother—or have a sherry.

She decided on the sherry. Really mother was becoming so tiresome these days. Sharp as a tack, no-one had expected Iris to get dementia, least of all Angie. At first it was annoying, but live-in home help had taken care of the forgetfulness and wandering down the street at all hours.

What they hadn't been able to control was the wandering of Iris's mind. That was the last straw. Angie had just finished organising a unit in an upmarket retirement home with 24 hour access to care. Moving her mother proved an exhausting process, but at least Iris was safe. She needed someone to keep an eye on her, and if it kept her outrageous statements out of the earshot of others, all the better.

Angie could still remember the shiver of shock that passed over her when she'd taken her mother out for lunch with a trio of her elderly friends. Iris had been a gentile delight. Until dessert arrived.

After sucking on her chocolate covered spoon (how Angie hated that habit) Iris cheerfully said, 'The skeletons will fall out of the closet one day. They always do. Dorothy, would you pass me the whipped cream, darling. This black forest cake is delicious. This dear little cafe is the best thing about Tenterfield. Don't you agree, Angie?'

Angie nearly choked. It took all of her composure to smooth over the remark. How carefully she hid their country origins. It would never do for the past to come tumbling down now. Who knew what her mother would say next? Angie breathed a sigh of relief when the conversation moved on to other topics. Not that she was a snob—never that. It's just that some things were best left in the past. She could just imagine her family unravelling.

What on earth had possessed her mother to use the word 'skeleton'? It was hardly a scandal, after all. She and James had just done what any decent Christian would do. They were the victims.

It was the living end when she dropped her mother home.

'Watch out for whispering hands, Ange,' said Iris.

'What? Really mother.'

'You know what I mean. You've seen them, Ange.'

"Ange" certainly had. She hated her name shortened by anyone other than James, but now wasn't the time for reproving her mother on *that* score. 'No, I don't mother! I don't understand you half the time anymore.'

'There is always something behind them.'

Angie was exasperated. She must end this conversation.

'Behind what, Mother?'

'Whispering hands.'

'Hands don't whisper, Mother. Only mouths do.'

'Same thing.'

Iris found herself relocated. Far enough away from her north shore friends to find the journey a little too much. It was all managed very nicely. All that was left to do was make the arrangement permanent. Just as well they had money to spare, and thankfully mother made no complaint about signing over the rent of her own unit to the retirement village. That left only half the fees for her and James to meet.

There was also some money coming through from the farm through mother's accountant. Angie was sure that was adequate for Iris's extras. She wouldn't want her mother to go short—she could still manage her cash. In fact, she was a little secretive about it. Never mind, things were sorted.

Mother was closer to them. And if the family actually visited less, no one was the wiser. Any visits always put Angie on edge—even when she went on her own, which she was doing more and more these days. It honestly made her teeth tingle just to hear her mother tell her new hostel friends that 'it will all end in tears, you mark my words'.

Goodness knows what Iris said when she wasn't there. Angie didn't want to know. All she had to do was separate the two worlds and all would be well. Her sister, Clare wouldn't object—not that there would be any use for her to try. Angie had long ago sorted her younger sister out, and their relationship was smooth, if somewhat cold. Sixteen years difference in their ages certainly helped.

If anyone, Lucy would be the fly in the ointment. As usual. Blundering into the middle of things with a thousand questions. Dragging life stories out of perfect strangers, then wearing out everyone's patience until they told her the real story. With ears that heard every whisper in the house. If she had a dollar for every time she heard, 'Lucy!' and then a loud 'What?' from Lucy she'd be a millionaire.

On more than one occasion Angie wondered if Lucy could read minds. The children joked she'd brought the wrong baby home from the hospital. Lucy, with her untamed, curly hair the colour of rich honey—unlike the rest of them with their straight-as-sticks pale blonde locks.

Lucy was slender like the rest of them, but she was like a tiny bird. They all towered over her, which made it very difficult for family photos. Especially when Lucy refused to stand on a stool and said, 'If you're all *that* ashamed of me just leave me out and pretend I'm the hired help.'

'No-one would hire you out to help with anything, Lucy Belmore. You should have been born with a personal maid. Your room is like a hurricane swept through it. I don't know how you can study in there,' said Ellie.

'Why do you have to be so difficult?' Angie persisted. These family photos made wonderful Christmas cards with that personal touch.

'Well, as I'm *not* ever studying housekeeping I doubt that I'll need that on my resume when I graduate. And I'm sure my height won't matter a damn when they take graduation photos. What a right fuss there would be then if someone insisted on stools for short people then. Perhaps they could make all the taller ones kneel down. Make the fat ones stand sideways and the thin ones flap their gowns out.'

Even peacemaker Sara had been goaded by this remark. 'Lucy Belmore, why does every simple thing turn into a debate with you? Why can't you be agreeable...?'

'...for once in my life,' ended Lucy, standing proud and straight where she was, causing the photographer to move back several feet and start all over again.

It was a good thing Lucy wouldn't be there tonight. She was hardly ever home these days. At 17 she'd rather 'die than hang out with Ellie's airbrushed friends.' Angie was happy to let her off attending the party, after all she'd behaved beautifully at the family birthday gathering during the week. Separate worlds.

She was off visiting Clare again. Angie originally had doubts about the idea, but she could count on Clare. Clare would hold her tongue though the heavens fell rather than have anyone hurt. She'd always been a bit sappy. Their mother often said that it was a weakness to let everyone walk over you, and Angie was in complete agreement with her mother for once.

However visiting Clare had worked out well, and now that Lucy was sixteen, she and James worried less. At first Clare had come to Sydney to travel on the train with Lucy. It certainly gave Lucy confidence, and the house was much quieter without her.

Angie was relieved that Ellie was enjoying her new job. Thankfully, her friends were a better class than before; although she was still fast friends with super-skinny Tatum Gregory.

She was sure Tatum fancied Robert, never missing a chance to flatter and flirt. Angie didn't want that vacuous girl getting her Robert. He paid far too much attention to her already.

At least his girlfriend Rachel would be there. He hadn't been going out with her for long, but they were so right for each other. Rachel was shy and sensible and would be a good wife and mother. An occupational therapist, she would be home instead of travelling the world.

She asked Sylvia about Tatum, hoping for some leverage. After all, Tatum was one of Sylvia's models, but Sylvia had merely said Tatum might party hard, but she worked hard as well, and didn't do drugs like some of the others. It hardly seemed like recommendation. Sylvia was obviously inured to the lifestyle of her girls. As long as they turned up to the photo shoot and pouted, it was fine.

With Tatum on the guest list, it was a good thing that Robert didn't usually stay long at family parties. He hardly fitted with his sisters' friends. Their antics made no sense to his reserved nature, and that was all for the better. She remembered him commenting that they were 'all beyond the pale' when Ellie's near disaster upset the family balance.

Angie rested her feet on the tapestry stool and let the afternoon breeze drift through the chiffon drapes. She sipped a little more of the sherry.

'Oh damn,' she yelped as the sherry glass hit the floor. Thank goodness it was the edge of the rug and there was little left. She must have gone to sleep. The doorbell rang again. Slipping elegant feet into her house shoes, Angie answered the door and ushered the caterers in, giving them the lists she had prepared that morning. One of the maids seemed to look at her a little longer than necessary, but then the girl had reached into her pocket and put on a pair of glasses. Angie sighed with relief.

She was worried about nothing. Thoughts of Tenterfield

tickled at the back of her mind. It was a strain always being on the lookout. If it wasn't her mother haunting her memories it was something else. She was almost relieved when she went to freshen up and noticed some of the sherry had spilled on her top, giving her time to regain her composure. Rubbing the mark furiously with one of the monogrammed towels in their upstairs ensuite she succeeded in removing the stain. But now her blouse was wrinkled. She was becoming like Lucy.

If James hadn't made that idiotic decision to work from home she would be happily ensconced in the parent's retreat off their bedroom instead of napping in the living room, sneaking a sherry. She made a mental note to breach the subject with him. Perhaps they could share the space. If she was really clever, she might even get him to work back in the city and use the room as it was designed, for a retreat—hers. Honestly, men needed so much managing. Although, with the rampant female hormones in the house it was a wonder James hadn't run screaming into the night. He really was a brick.

There was one consolation—Ellie had come out of the pregnancy scare situation focused and mature, and none of their social set was any the wiser, apart from Sylvia of course. That was all in the past. Ellie had a new job. It had been such a relief when she'd landed a wonderful reception job in a medical research centre after finishing the office administration course. And there was Brian Fenton. Everything she'd ever wanted for Ellie.

The party went like a dream. Ellie and Brian looked so happy together. She wouldn't be surprised if they were engaged soon. Drifting off to sleep that night, her mind wandered to suitable plans for an engagement party.

Angie rose in the morning with a new sense of optimism. Taking an extra sleeper had ensured a wonderful sleep. She was even ready for her visit to her mother. She must get another prescription—shame the doctor was becoming a little concerned about her use. Never mind, she'd visit one of Sylvia's doctors again. She had a list for her models.

Humming as she warmed the BMW up, she felt she could face anything.

As she entered the Low Care facility with her handbag jauntily over her shoulder, the Manager's secretary approached her, with her customary clipboard and that inscrutable smile she wore.

'Could you please come into the office for just a moment Mrs Belmore? Thank you.'

The woman walked towards the office, her heels clicking officiously. Angie ground her teeth. The woman annoyed her. She took compliance for granted. What if it hadn't suited her? What if she had some important appointment?

She sat obediently in the chair, leaning forward as she waited, hoping that gave the impression of a busy woman not to be kept waiting. At least in that, she was rewarded. The manager came through and ushered Angie into her office.

Before Angie had time to sit down she announced, 'There is a problem with your mother's payments.'

'What ... that can't be. They've been coming out of her account automatically from the rent from her unit. There must be a mistake, surely. There are funds from the farm in Tenterfield.'

'That may be so, but there are new arrangements. We've been contacted by your mother's power of attorney, a Mr John Collins, and...'

Angie Belmore fainted.

David

Dave swallowed. Clenching the glass, bitterness burned like bile. How had things turned out this badly? He'd just had an idyllic week fishing and camping with the guys. Not normally his thing, they'd talked him into it. Insisted. Most of them were guys who worked for him.

'You shouldn't be alone after a divorce, Dave,' Mike had said, helping him pack. 'Not a sappy softie like you. Now that I think of it—you shouldn't be on the loose at all, never mind at home on your own.'

It had been a week of laughter, sunburn, silly races and sheer fun. Something he couldn't remember doing for a long, long time. Sitting around the fire at night had been a spiritual experience—not that he would ever tell them that.

Jimbo brought a leash along—labelled "DAVE'S LEASH", and they'd had a ceremonial burning, along with a silly dance.

Mike made a rambling speech. 'We all hope our mate Dave has enough sense to move on, up or anywhere except with the bitch he married, but there's hope now he's divorced the manipulating article.'

They were terrific guys. Not for the first time, Dave Richards wondered why his working relationships surpassed his personal and family ones.

Dave had laughed 'til his stomach hurt. If a few random tears rolled down his face in the dark of night, no one knew. Some of the sadness was for Estella, but he'd fallen out of love with her. The tears were for what could have been. Tears for a childless marriage.

He loved Jamie, Estella's son, like his own, but it had always been a dream to have a child of his own. They'd tried for years before giving up. He blamed himself. After all, Estella had no trouble falling pregnant in her first marriage.

'There's no point in exhaustive tests,' Estella said. 'It's just not meant to be, darling.'

Dave hadn't wanted to push for adoption. Estella wasn't keen; she didn't want Jamie to feel second best. Never mind her husband feeling second best.

Dave gave the phone an angry look as if he could take back time. Undo pressing the answering machine button. Unhear what he'd heard.

Before listening to the messages he'd been basking in the holiday aura, wanting to stretch it out. The decree nisi sat on the table in front of him. His freedom. Or so he'd thought. The third message on the answering machine had undone him.

He supposed he should be grateful that Estella hadn't phoned herself, but somehow it was worse hearing it from her sister, Serena. The 'Estella doesn't want you to know' line hadn't fooled him one bit; she was probably in the room at the time. Guilt gnawed at him like a tooth deciding whether to ache. False guilt—but that didn't matter. Estella had cervical cancer. She was in Hillside Public, recovering from a hysterectomy, and would begin chemotherapy as soon as she was discharged.

How ironic, he thought, downing the last of his bourbon. A hysterectomy. The removal of her womb. The final act in their childless saga. But all of that paled in the light of Serena's last sentence, 'Well, at least you didn't sign the divorce papers, Dave. Not that...well, you know...I don't mean to...Oh I hate these machines...' Beep.

How could Estella not know that the divorce had gone through? She'd initiated it. She'd thrown down the divorce papers in her usual theatrical style.

'I don't want to be dramatic, darling. We both know this

isn't working. Your work is your passion. You sacrificed any lifestyle we could have enjoyed for it. If only you'd swallowed your pride and worked in your family business. I've waited long enough for you to come to your senses, but even now, with the death of your father, you show no interest in joining the company that is your birthright.'

In the space of time it took to buy an airline ticket online, she was gone. He really believed she meant it, had wanted a divorce, but now doubts were niggling at him. Had the whole thing been a grandiose ploy to get him to tow the line? Shut down his business and join the family company? He'd never been inclined towards his father's business. Fast talking real estate deals weren't his thing. He'd have been useless. His sales ability was non-existent. It was more his brother's style, and Paul had happily run the business for years. There was no tension between the brothers.

The expectation was in Estella's mind. Of course, his father had made his disappointment clear, but 'disappointment' from his father was par for the course. He'd learned to live with that fact decades ago. He couldn't remember a time when he'd succeeded in pleasing the old man.

Why was Estella acting as if there was still a marriage? She should have received the paperwork too. But when he thought about it, it made complete sense, really. Estella had spent the last year traipsing around the world. There was no doubt about it, this new development with Estella made for a very sticky situation. Dave knew what the guys would say. He should leave well enough alone, but he knew no matter much he tried to ignore the situation, he wouldn't. There was something unfinished.

Another thing was unfinished. The bottle of bourbon. He reached for it.

'Planning to down the lot are you, Dad?' It was Jamie.

'Yes, son. That's the plan.'

'It's not like you to drink at all. I take it you've heard about Mum.'

'Uh-huh.'

'Does she know the divorce has gone through?'

'Not according to Serena.'

'Bah—Serena. What's she doing? Still trying to get close to her big sister? She's wasting her time. Mum only uses people. Including you, Dad. Look at you, you look terrible. I always admired that you didn't touch that stuff. She has a bad effect on you. I hope you're not having second thoughts.'

'I don't like you talking about her like that Jamie.' Dave flinched.

'I'm an adult, Dad, not a child. I know her. Why do you think I moved in with you when she wanted to go overseas?'

'As if! You were already here,' Dave laughed. 'And I see

you most days at work.'

'Come on, Dad—without me your wrought iron masterpieces would still be sitting in the workshop. Together we make magic. I'm your best landscape designer.'

'You're my *only* landscape designer.'

'Ergo.'

'So, have you been to see your mother?'

Jamie looked solemn. 'Yeah. I love her, you know that. It doesn't mean I have to convince myself that she's an angel— if she hadn't married you, I'd have been passed from Aunt Serena to Gran and Pop, then back again,' he said. 'My guess is that you'll go and see her.'

'Yeah.'

'Well, when you do...'

'Hey! Enough already. How's my company? Didn't burn the place down while I was away, did you?'

"Course not. I left my pyromaniac phase at fifteen.'

'So, how are things there? Anything new?'

'Janice has organised some interviews for the workroom assistant's position. She's got half a dozen lined up for you to interview tomorrow.'

'That soon,' said Dave, suddenly tired. 'At least I'll have...'

'...a good night's sleep,' finished Jamie. 'You and your 'good night's sleep' before everything. I don't think you've ever made an on-the-spot decision in your life.'

'Nature of the beast.'

'Yeah, well. Leave the grog alone or I'll throw it down the sink.'

'Chuck the lot out, I don't care—it's only made me depressed.'

Jamie smiled. 'I love ya, Dad.'

'Thanks. I love you too.'

Dave's good night's sleep didn't eventuate. He was awake till all hours thinking about Estella. He saw no way out other than to take care of her. When he did sleep, his dreams were chaotic and he woke not only tired, but cranky.

Even though he didn't feel up to it, he had to turn up to work for the interviews. It wasn't fair to the interviewees. Arriving early at the office he drank several cups of coffee and put a smile on his face. He could at least act human. He didn't bother to read the résumés before the interviews. There wasn't time. Anyway, they'd never know. He'd pose a few questions and let them do the talking.

His secretary, Janice, was a godsend, giving the hopeful applicants a job description and ushering them in. And no one else could work magic with their temperamental coffee machine. Thank God she kept those coming.

He took a quick break. All those coffees had worked—he needed the bathroom. He slipped into the hallway. There was a slim girl with long blonde hair leaning over her backpack in the waiting area. Great. A teenager.

Janice ushered the girl in on his return. She smiled.

'Oh my God!' said Dave, *'Clare?'*

Estella

'Oh Serena, help me with my make-up. I know I shouldn't have expected it, but I hoped Dave might come straight away. After you phoned. Four days I've waited. Four days, and still no sign of him,' said Estella, as she rummaged through her cosmetics bag. 'Help me, darling. I don't want to look like an old hag. God, what havoc anaesthetics wreak on one's skin.'

'I wouldn't get my hopes up, Estella. A year can change a man.'

'Not Dave,' said Estella, 'Of course, I'll understand if he takes a while to think about it. He's never been one to rush into anything. But he'll come back to me. I can make him love me again.'

'Even when he finds out you've spent all your money?'

'How many times have I told you I was swindled? It's not my fault. I have too much faith in people. It's always been a failing of mine.'

Behind her, Serena rolled her eyes, thankful her sister couldn't see because she was absorbed in the mirror. 'Well, you might actually find you've put too much faith in your power over Dave.'

Estella burst into tears.

Serena hugged her. *Oh dear, here comes Act II.* She sighed, wiped Estella's tears, and said she was sorry. After all, her sister was very ill. She would have to be more sensitive. Bite her tongue. At least Estella noticed her existence now. It might be a chance to mend fences.

'If I didn't know any better I'd think you were jealous of Dave and I,' said Estella. 'Why are you being such a cow?'

So much for mending fences, thought Serena. 'Graeme and I are perfectly happy. I'm a lucky woman. Now, just lie back and I'll give you a facial.'

'With the hot towel treatment?'

'Yes, with the hot towel. Do you want a mask?'

'Gosh no, I don't want to look like something from the bottom of a swamp.' Estella grimaced.

'I'll only do this if you promise to relax,' said Serena.

'Thank you, darling. You are so good to me. How was I so lucky to have you for a sister? A beautician, with your own little business.'

Serena ignored the slight. After all, with Estella's financial situation it might be better if she thought of her sister as a small time shop owner. There was no need to tell her that she had four boutique stores that were thriving.

When she first came to Estella's side, Serena would have told her everything and offered her the world, but after a week of her sister's mercurial mood changes and barbed insults—she had second thoughts. The last thing she wanted now was for Estella to decide to move in with her and take over her life. Her hopes for a warm sisterly connection were fading fast.

It's just that Estella could be so sweet and funny. Serena had always envied her ease with people and her ability to bond with them effortlessly. As for her ability to get what she wanted—well, that wasn't to be envied—it hurt innocent people like Dave. Serena was secretly delighted that he hadn't come running like he usually did. It would be better if he didn't show at all, but he was tied to Estella by the same desperate hope as she.

Mind you, for all of Estella's people manoeuvring, she was here in a public hospital ward. Her finances must be drastically low to end up in a public hospital. Even then, she'd been able to somehow finagle a private room by a combination of Bambi eyes and complaints.

Serena thought of the last time Estella had been in a public hospital. How often she'd been tempted to tell Dave about that, but sisterly loyalty had won out in the end. One lie seemed so little then. Serena was only a teenager and had no idea that one lie would become years of deception.

Serena's heart sank. There was Dave at the nurses' station. A fleeting instinct to tell him to walk away tugged at her, but she was frozen. Looking through the narrow gap in the doorway, she tensed.

'What is it?' Estella asked.

Serena sighed. 'It's Dave,' she said.

'Oh good,' said Estella. 'I knew he'd come.'

Dave didn't seem to be in a hurry. He was talking with the sister.

'Serena, for goodness sake sit down! I don't need you standing there gawking at him. Act casual. Then when he comes, say you have to get a vase or something, and leave us.'

'You don't need a vase.'

Estella grabbed the bunch of flowers Serena had brought, took them out of the vase, thumped them on the overbed table, then put the vase in the bedside drawer and slammed it shut. 'Now we do!' she said.

Arranging herself artistically on the bed with the nurse call bell in her hand, Estella lay back with a gentle moan.

'He's not here yet!' hissed Serena, becoming tired of the charade. She sat down in the corner.

'What the blazes is he doing? Are you sure it's him? You are short-sighted Serena.'

'I'm long-sighted, Estella, which you'd know if you knew me at all. And yes, it is him. I've known him as long as you have, *remember*?'

'You don't care that I'm dying.'

'With chemo you have a good prognosis, Estella. And I'm here, aren't I? When everyone else had deserted you.'

'I'm sorry darling, it's this blasted cancer talking,' purred Estella. 'Get up and see what's going on.'

'You just told me to!'

'Pretty please.'

Serena moaned softly. Estella favoured her with the 'you're such hard work' look that she was so familiar with, but she complied. 'He's talking with the sister.'

'Oh dear man, he's asking how I'm doing. Which sister?'

'The one that was in here before.'

'Oh no, not Sister O'Connell. She's a right cow. Said I was having too much pain relief and being too demanding of the nurses. Said she had dying patients to attend to—doesn't she know I'm dying. Doesn't she read the blasted notes herself?'

'You're not dying, Estelle.'

'Don't you call me that again ... ever! No one knows I changed my name. It's Estella.' She pronounced the word slowly.

'...so you could sound exotic and Mediterranean ... not plain old Estelle Abbot from Broken Hill who married Joe

Martinez from Campbelltown.'

Estella sniffed. 'He's half Italian.'

'Who can't speak a word of it.' Serena sighed and fluffed the pillows. 'Anyway, you're not dying. You only have to have one round of chemo, and that's if you decide to have the extra 'protection' because you wailed so much. The surgeon was very pleased he got all the cancer. So I guess one could say that you don't even have cancer anymore. It's in the rubbish. A positive attitude is what you need.'

'Why isn't Dave in here? He's taking ages. What's he doing?'

'Reading.'

'What? What's he reading?'

'I can't see.'

'Oh, he's probably reading my notes and he'll see how much I've suffered and want to take care of me like he always did. If those nurses have written anything nasty I'll sue them. Slander, I'll have them.'

'The sister is with him,' said Serena.

'What! The old bat could be telling him anything. No, she wouldn't. They have to worry about confidentiality.'

'Not with one's husband. They can tell him anything.'

'But the divorce went through...oh damn...'

'What! You didn't tell me that! You and Dave are divorced!'

'Don't you breathe a word...'

'I told him...I thought, he hadn't signed them. You told me he' hadn't signed!'

'Well, I didn't think he would.'

'You practically threw the papers at him.'

'I was hoping he'd wake up.'

'Really! Was he asleep?'

'Sarcasm is uncalled for, Serena.'

'Estella, what have you done? I feel a complete fool. I told him that it was...well, good that you were still married and he hadn't done anything hasty—because you told me nothing had happened.'

'What else could I tell you?'

'Well gee, Estella, I don't know—the truth maybe.'

Estella waved her arm dismissively. 'Keep your eye on him. What's keeping him now?'

'He's still reading.'

'Where's Sister Mussolini?'

'Gone,' said Serena, 'Oh, she's back now—with a folder.'

'That better not be private. Oh, it's probably cancer care notes for relatives. Dear, sweet Dave. He thinks of everything. I don't know why that used to annoy me. The pernickety perfectionism. He'll be such a good carer.'

'You've only got six weeks of recovery from the surgery, three months at the most.'

'Unless I have chemo...'

'Oh, you wouldn't lie about that, would you Estella? Not even you...'

'Men need some...you know...help to feel real sympathy for others...Oh don't look at me like that.'

'Sh! He's coming!' said Serena, hastily sitting down and picking up a magazine.

'You could make yourself...' She turned to the door and waved a weal arm. 'Dave, darling.'

'Estella,' said Dave, his voice cool.

Estella gave him a weak smile, which faded when she saw the folder. It was her medical records folder. Panic flitted across her face. She struggled to keep her cool. No. How could that bitch sister get her old medical records?

'Dave?'

'Estella.'

Estella's heart raced. She'd never seen Dave like this—so cold towards her. Not even in their worst fight. He'd never been one to say much, but this?

'Oh Dave, you must have a few words for me, at least.'

'I do.'

'Memories...' sang Estella, trying to lighten the mood, 'I remember when you first said those words...' She stopped abruptly. Dave's face was positively stormy.

'I will regret those words for the rest of my life,' he said.

'But we're not div...'

'Oh yes we are, and I'd bet anything that you know.'

Estella flushed. 'But Dave...'

He held up the file. 'But that's just one of your deceptions, isn't it?'

Words choked in Estella's throat.

'Here are some words I have for you—"tubal ligation"—don't worry; the sister was good enough to explain. You were sterilised. There was no chance of a child. When I think of all the discussions we had, deciding. When all the time there was no possibility. None!'

'But Dave...that was before...'

'It was *after* we became engaged. You said you were caring for Serena who had Glandular Fever.'

Serena didn't move. She was afraid to breathe.

'Did you have Glandular Fever, Serena?'

Serena shook her head.

Dave turned to Estella.

She folded her arms and glared at him. She would not be humiliated. 'Is that all you have to say, Dave?'

'No, I have two more words.'

Estella waited, her eyes like fire.

'Decree nisi.' He was gone.

Estella wailed like a wounded animal.

Serena handed her the box of tissues. Estella clung to her.

'At least I have you, Sis.'

Serena blanched. She remembered how sweet her husband Graeme had been about bringing Estella home, even if it would turn their lives upside down. She went through a mental list of her friends. Surely one of them would know of a health resort where she could organise Estella to convalesce. It would be worth the money.

She'd heard of a few that didn't allow phone contact.

Arthur

Heavy footsteps crunched on the gravel. Millie tensed, then walked faster. The steps behind her took up the pace.

'Millie,' said a voice, 'walk this way.'

'Arthur...wha...' Millie's throat was tight.

'The press are here. They're camped out at the end of the cul de sac.' Arthur linked her arm through his and covered her with his umbrella. 'Keep walking. Come with me to my wife's grave. That will throw them off—vultures!'

'Oh, thank...' Tears streamed down Millie's face. Sheltered by an acquaintance. It was too much after the past few weeks with friends deserting her in droves. She faced a torrent of abuse every time she left the house. Camera crews outside the high walled fence of their home. Those walls would not protect her from this present storm.

Slowly and calmly Arthur steered Millie to the lawn

section of the cemetery. Millie stood frozen to the spot while Arthur reached into his ample black coat and took out a plastic bag. It was filled with white rose petals. Millie was soothed by the simple ritual of Arthur spreading the petals. The fine mist of rain made them shine like diamonds on the well mown lawn.

'I'm sorry you have to go through all that.' Arthur tilted his head towards the blue van.

'I don't know why you're being so nice. I'm a piranha now. Untouchable. Persona non gratis.'

'I was there that day. In the hospital.'

'I know. I saw you. I actually wondered if it was you who phoned the press.'

'Oh, no! I was there doing a survey for research into breast cancer. My wife, you had it, you know.'

'It must have been a visitor, someone random. I was so sure the staff wouldn't. They'd be afraid of losing their jobs. But I suppose the temptation for *this* story was just too great. For some money hungry coward. The Mayor fighting for his life in the midst of false allegations.'

'Not quite how I read it...' Arthur murmured.

'No. Not even close. That's what we would have released to the press. If we'd had a chance. But the press were on the scene like fleas on a dog. They even got photos of Mark being taken to Intensive Care on the trolley with tubes and monitors. No dignity. At least they didn't get pictures of the rope burns on his neck. Don't they care about...have any humanity.' Millie was furious. Arthur fell silent.

'Mark is such...was...such a loving husband. To be accused of sexual assault—they might as well have said rape. There's no way he was a sex addict, or whatever they're claiming. Most undemanding man on the earth. Always kept me informed of his whereabouts, fussy to a fault about that although I never asked. You don't, if you have trust, you know? He had years of hell when that wretched Katie Morris went to the police and had him charged. Took her two years to decide to come forward. How very convenient. Suspicious, I say. Mark held his head high over that and didn't slow down. He was elected by the people of this town, and he's worked damn hard for them.'

Arthur was feeling uncomfortable. He expected a grieving widow, but Millie was angry. He knew little of the Mayor—didn't concern himself with politics. A good Sunday paper and the sports section and he was happy. Of course, he couldn't fail to hear about the scandal, but he was not a man to judge others quickly.

It was raining heavier now, but Millie showed no sign of slowing down. He wished he could call someone. There were four daughters. If only he could remember something about them. Anything at all.

'Millie, can I call one of your daughters?'

'It was when the others decided to get on the bandwagon that he was hit hard. And ... now ... I'll never see him walk through the door again. Our eldest is having her first baby. Mark never lived to even know. He would have made a good grandfather...'

'Millie, where are your daughters? Ah, Sally ... um ... doesn't she work at the bank?'

'The girls are shattered. What do I tell them? Oh, God. I can't do this.' Millie howled. 'And I can't even visit his grave. I'm standing here at a stranger's grave. They can't do this to me. I won't let them.'

She ran across the cemetery, back to the fresh mound of earth, and knelt in the soft soil, moaning and rocking back and forth. The rain bucketed down.

The reporters exploded out of the van. A tall redhead with a clipboard over her head gestured for the cameraman to hurry up. As soon as they arrived he began snapping. A third man carried a gym bag and two umbrellas, handing one to the redhead, shielding the cameraman with the other. He looked about fourteen. He dropped the gym bag, hitting the cameraman with the umbrella as he reached down to retrieve it.

'For God's sake, Jason!' yelled the red-faced cameraman.

Millie was no longer aware of her surroundings. Her hair

was dishevelled and her face covered in streaks of mud where she'd swiped at her red rimmed eyes.

Arthur threw his coat over her.

'My God, you people are animals!' He said, pulling on the redhead's arm. 'Listen Missie, you or one of your minions had better tell me the phone number of one of her daughters. The way you've been scavenging around this family you should know their every detail. Leave off mate, put that camera away.'

The redhead shrugged, punched a number into her mobile, handed it to him then continued to throw questions at Millie.

'How do you feel about your husband's betrayal, Mrs Henderson? Were you aware of his sexual exploits? The voters want answers.'

Millie continued to rock and murmur.

A few words were all that Arthur needed to say to Millie's daughter, Sally—she was already on her way. She had intended to meet her mother there, but was delayed. She was minutes away.

Arthur quietly took both of the crew's umbrellas and headed for their van.

'Jeez, mate. We'll have you for that! You can't steal from us!' yelled the cameraman.

'Don't you dare touch that car you idiot!' screeched the

redhead. 'We can film you doing it—talk about stupid!'

'The camera's drenched,' said the cameraman, 'We've lost the whole morning's work—and possibly the camera. Why'd you let him take the umbrellas right out of your hands, you dimwit? Do you have any idea how much this equipment costs? Chase the bastard!'

The youth looked from one to the other.

Across the street Arthur folded the umbrellas, opened the van door, threw them in then locked the door.

'Oh no!' howled the assistant. 'The keys are in the car!'

Arthur stood on the other side of the road. Sally flew around the corner into the car park. He waved. She sped towards them. Arthur smiled. She would be unlikely to offer the unfortunate trio assistance. Of any kind.

Clare

Clare hummed as she wandered through the Sydney Art Gallery. It was so exciting to be part of a major exhibition at last. There was something surreal about walking around seeing your own work among the best of your peers. The exhibition was a wonderful celebration of art and sculpture. The vibe inside just buzzed.

She was particularly interested to see how her mosaic discs had been combined with the work of another artist who specialised in wrought iron. At last she found her contributions. There was the table she had scribbled some ideas for the craftsman.

The result was beyond her dreams. She had combined mosaic work with coloured resins to create a translucent colour wash over the mosaic. The wrought iron artist had captured the essence of her work and matched the colours and elegance of her design. Some of the smaller discs, with similar effects, had been used randomly in a stone wall. That was something she hadn't expected.

The lighting in the gallery was spectacular. The high ceilings produced a wonderful perspective on the art, that couldn't have been achieved in the smaller galleries where she'd previously shown her work.

'It's marvellous to be able to touch the work, don't you think?' said a young man. He seemed in his mid-twenties. 'It makes for a more visceral experience.'

'I didn't think you were allowed to touch the works,' said Clare, a little affronted.

'Ah. Yes. But I helped set this area up. Pardon me, I'm Jamie Martinez.' Jamie smiled widely, and offered his hand. 'In fact, that is my stone wall over there. Of course, the real artist is the woman who created the discs. Aren't they wonderful?'

Clare smiled. 'I'm Clare,' she said. 'In fact they're my discs.' She gave him a brief handshake.

'Oh, so you're *dreamcatchers*', that's terrific. Are you pleased with the results? My father made the wrought iron work.'

'Yes, there's true genius in meeting my original brief, yet adding something unique, something special.'

'I'll tell him that, he will be touched. He doesn't attend

these things; he prefers the workshop.'

'His work is familiar somehow...I'm not sure...hmm...' Clare shrugged. 'I'm probably imagining it.'

'Well, it was a real pleasure to meet you, Clare. I have to meet someone. Enjoy the rest of your day.'

Jamie smiled, and left. How fortunate to meet Clare. How interesting. He checked his watch, he'd better be on time for the girls he thought of as Lucretia Borgia. The way Sara talked about her sister Lucy, it might have been easier to meet the big, bad wolf in Grandma's house.

Clare was thrilled with the table. There was something indefinable about the style of work that stirred memories. It was special.

Usually she didn't mind parting with her pieces, but this one was different. She'd worked hard to make a living out of her art, but for once she resented having to sell. There was no choice with this one though. The other craftsman, the young man's father, had rights over the collaboration too. She simply couldn't afford to pay the extra to keep it. By going without new clothes and appliances she could save— she'd long ago accepted that these were sacrifices she had to make.

Pregnant at sixteen, then falling ill—unable to go back to school, had added up to tough times. The pain of handing her baby over had eased, but never dissolved. Taking the art course at the new wave art school had given her a second chance at following her dreams, and a place to try and adjust to trauma of the past. Sometimes she wondered if watching her daughter from a distance was worse than knowing nothing.

Picking up a few sandwiches, Clare wandered the room, lost in a world of her own.

Remembering.

Remembering young sweet love. He'd been such a shy city boy. Pale, and uncoordinated—at least with farm chores. But not with the junk he welded into fantasy art. And not with her.

Six weeks of bliss was all they had known. No one existed but the other. At the end of his time there he had been tanned and fit, playful and fun loving. In her father Ralph, he found the acceptance and calm tolerance lacking in his own home. He'd been adamant. He couldn't wait to come back to the farm and leave city life behind. His father had sent him to the farm to sort him out, but he'd found his genius and true self instead. How she'd loved him. She had believed him. She'd waited.

He didn't come. The weight on her chest made her feel she might die.

Then the joy of the birth of her pink cheeked child. The haemorrhage that nearly claimed her life. The emptiness had felt like a life sentence. In hell. He didn't write, her options, her future—were gone.

Shaking herself, she realised she was late for lunch with Sara and Lucy. Just as well they were just across the road. Flipping her orange summer scarf over her shoulder she ran, arriving out of breath at the table.

'Hello Sara,' she said. 'Where's Lucy...?'

Once lowered into the nearest chair, Clare could see a man seated with Sara, hidden by the abundant foliage of one of the large potted plants.

He stood.

'Oh my! *Dave?*'

Jamie

'I don't know, Sara,' said Jamie, 'I mean, is all this clandestine stuff really necessary?'

'You don't know Lucy.'

'She sounds fearsome. Are you sure I won't be in any danger?'

'Sh! Here she comes now...Hi Lucy...'

'Hi Sara. You have your guilty face. Why do you look like you've just joined the Manson family?'

'She's everything you said and more,' muttered Jamie. This earned him a thump on the arm from Sara.

'This is Jamie,' said Sara, 'he's my boss's stepson and...'

'...landscaping genius,' added Jamie, holding out his hand.

'I'm so *very* pleased to meet you, Jamie,' said Lucy, shaking the hand he extended.

'You're a dreadful liar,' said Jamie.

'I know—it's a rare gift. I shall be getting the Order of Australia for it soon,' Lucy said, then turned to Sara. 'As much as I enjoy meeting Prince Charming here, where's Aunt Clare? I thought we were meeting her for lunch after she'd been to her exhibition.'

'Look Lucy, I need to see Clare in private, understand?'

'No,' said Lucy, 'not at all. Heard of telephones, Sara? Visiting on your own? Why heck, there are lots of options other than bringing your sister halfway across the city for no good reason.'

'There's a good reason. I just can't tell you yet.'

'You *have* joined the Manson family.' Lucy crossed her arms.

'Jamie will take you for a while...'

'Oh, white slavery is it? Organ harvesting, perhaps? Overseas prostitution?'

'Lucy, please! Don't be difficult. Just this once.'

'Why do people say just this once when they've done it a hundred times? Can't you count?'

'I'll owe you, I promise. Jamie will enjoy buying you lunch,' Sara begged.

'He looks like he'd rather go to a public hanging—his own,' said Lucy.

'Would you rather see the workshop?' asked Jamie. This

was going to be harder than he thought.

'What workshop? I don't think so. Lead on McDuff—where's the food?'

'You don't know about the workshop?'

'No, but you can tell me over lunch. I'll be better able to escape your ruthless clutches if I have something in my stomach.' Lucy slipped her arm through his, and smiled.

'You know, when you grow up—you're going to be...'

'...trouble, I know, everyone says...'

'Quite beautiful,' Jamie said.

'Oh...Thank you.'

After ordering they sat and chatted. Jamie was surprised by Lucy's calm acceptance of the arrangement. He had a feeling it was too soon to tell.

'Jamie, this is for you, mate,' said one of the waiters, handing him an auction slip. 'How's the gardening business going?'

Jamie put his foot out and the waiter sidestepped it.

'Come here often?' asked Lucy.

'Isn't that supposed to be my line?'

'You've used your only good line. So you bought something at the exhibition?' Lucy picked up the brochure and the slip with the number of his purchase on it. 'Really, so you bought my aunt's table? Good taste.'

'How did you...?'

Lucy shrugged.

'Are you psychic too?'

'Of course. I'm wondering—who is that man with my aunt and Sara?'

'What the...? How...?'

'They do keep the glass windows in this place pristine, don't you think? It's a credit to the place.'

Jamie sunk his head into his hands. 'Not psychic then.'

'Oh ye who doubt.'

'Will you read my palm?'

Lucy took his hand. 'I see chicanery.'

'Who?'

'And deception, thinly disguised.'

'Really.'

'And prevarication.'

'You don't say...'

'I do,' said Lucy, dropping his hand suddenly. 'And if you don't come clean and tell me why I'm stuck here with you, so that my sister, my aunt and some stranger are sitting a few metres away—leaving me with the worst spy in history, you're lifeline will be very short. Comprendez?'

Jamie sighed. 'I guess you'll find out anyway. Can you keep a secret?'

'No.'

Jamie rolled his eyes.

'Good,' said Lucy, 'I'll just go and ask them.' Her gaze was determined, his eyes beseeched her. She began to rise. He put his arm out to her. She hesitated.

Just then the food arrived. The aroma of pasta tickled her senses. 'After I've had...this divine looking Bolognese.' She attacked her food heartily.

Jamie was grateful she'd acquiesced.

'So, is everything all right? With them...?' Her eyes were vulnerable.

'No. But I think it will be in time.'

'Ah. Honesty suits you.'

'Thank you.'

'Maybe I'm better off not knowing.'

'That doesn't seem in your nature.'

'It's not, but...if they need to talk, then I won't pry.'

Jamie looked into her clear green eyes, and knew what it cost her to trust him. Sara would need her, there would be ripples that would rock the family. 'Sara is your cousin...I don't know how to say this...'

Lucy sat stock still. 'Cous...Oh, I don't think you need to...' Tears pricked at her eyes. She sniffled. Jamie handed her his handkerchief. 'I'm sorry, hot food always does this...oh dear...this will...'

Jamie put his hand gently over hers and told her what he knew. Clare and Dave had met when he'd gone to their farm to experience some of life's rough and tumble as part of his father's scheme to get him to wake up to himself.

'But how could he leave her...like that?'

'He came back, but was warned off, quite thoroughly apparently. Dad never knew about Sara. He was shocked that Clare was only sixteen when he knew her.'

'He's *your* father too? So, we're like *related*?'

'Oh no...No! He married my mother when I was eight—he's been a brilliant dad, though.'

'I can't eat any more,' said Lucy, pushing the half-finished food aside. 'And the table?' she touched the docket.

'It's from Dad to Sara. He's thrilled—he always wanted a child of his own. He adores her.'

'He's suffered the most then.'

'I guess. It's very generous of you to see it that way.'

'Well, he was the only one without a choice.'

Jamie told her about Sara applying for work and what had transpired at the interview. Sara wanted to sort things with Clare before doing anything hasty.

'That's Sara all right. Always calm,' said Lucy, 'but this time... I don't know.'

They sat in silence for a while, each digesting the future. In their own separate worlds.

'How did you manage to see them in the glass?'

'Dad paid for laser surgery because he was sick of paying

for my glasses. They used to just call me big ears but now they've added bionic eyes.'

Jason laughed. 'You're one of a kind, Lucy Belmore. A breath of fresh air.'

'Ah, you don't know me yet.'

'I can't wait to address that gap in my knowledge base.'

'Do you want to date me, Jamie Martinez?'

'We're on our first date now, aren't we?' he said.

Lucy's eyes sparkled. 'Oh my goodness. The mind boggles at what on earth you could do to top this. Here I am with a dodgy would-be-spy, who has practically kidnapped me. What next?' Lucy tilted her head.

Jamie thought how beautiful she was when she was teasing him. In fact, he couldn't imagine a time when she wouldn't be gorgeous.

Nothing seemed to faze her, which was so attractive. An engaging nature, along with a quick wit, and he was...well...gone. He knew she was intelligent and caring. Sara had told him about her studies in social work.

This "chore" had turned out rather well.

He'd thank Sara later. From her, Jamie had learned of Lucy's love and protectiveness of her family and that she enjoyed the community work in her course. He could just imagine her no-nonsense approach combined with that optimistic warmth and compassion she hid under a layer of nonchalance.

'Really, though. You're lovely. Enchanting. I would like another date...I mean, a real one. I promise not to ask you to marry me for at least six months. What more can a girl ask for?'

'Just as long as you know I've had my heart set on eloping, which won't be easy with a three storey house.'

Jamie touched her face. 'I'll get a fire truck.'

Lucy blushed.

He laughed. 'So you really are the perfect woman?'

'Oh dear, we'll end in disaster if you hang on to that illusion.'

Robert

'I have to tell you that it doesn't look good, Dad. You don't have many options. The credit crisis has hit hard.' Robert loosened his tie. He and his father had been going over the company books on and off for two days now, locked up in James' home office.

'I'm beginning to see that, son.'

'Well, the sooner you act, the less you'll lose. Sit on this lot and you face bankruptcy.' Robert tapped the papers on the desk.

'That is grim.'

'Does mother know how bad things are? When does she get home?'

'Who knows? She's out a lot lately. I've tried to tell her about the money situation but she says I'm a worrywart. I can't get through to her. I wish her brother John had handled

93

things better. He took Iris back to her unit and set her up with a live-in companion. Then Angie found out that he has power of attorney. He paid her back the money we put into the unit promptly enough, but he told her he wouldn't sit down and talk to her until she'd calmed down. You don't tell Angie that! She's been like a bear with a sore head ever since. She put the money, *our money* I might add, into her account and went mad with it. Shopping! I've never seen such shopping. She can't seem to stop.

'Well, you have to act, Dad. Cut off her credit.'

'She would fall apart, she's already on the brink of a breakdown—the secret coming out about Sara not being our daughter but Clare's nearly killed your mother, added to the rest—God, I don't know. Sara won't come home. Won't return our calls.'

'Give her time,' said Robert, resisting the impulse to check his watch, again.

He thought of Tatum waiting at home. He didn't come here to listen to his father's emotional ramble. All he could see was that it would have been a lot simpler if his parents had been forthcoming in the first place.

'We thought we were doing the best thing taking Sara. Maybe we could have been a bit better about Clare seeing her, but who wants their child upset? God, listen to me.' James ran his fingers through his hair. 'I'm concerned. Your mother's blood pressure is through the roof. I'm worried she'll have a stroke.'

'I'd be more worried about her drinking.'

'So you've noticed?'

'Everyone has, Dad. They're just not saying anything. Sara said mother was tipsy in the early afternoon months back.'

'Sara? Not Lucy? It must be bad then.'

'Don't underestimate Sara, Dad. She's a dark horse. I don't think she misses anything. She just likes to stay under the radar.'

James struggled to take it all in. He hardly knew where to start. It seemed that all of his children knew more about what was going on in his house then he did.

'Well, we've become a complete zoo. Iris diagnosed with mild schizophrenia, then a second opinion says it's not that—she's diabetic with mild forgetfulness and recurring 'bladder something'. Angie's apparently hitting the bottle, Ellie is house-sharing in the city with that Denton boy and another couple. Cheap way to live together and pretend they're not to keep up appearances. Sara is working with Dave—living God knows where. You moved out to live with Tatum. And to top it off our money's almost gone,' he said.

Robert put his pen down with a thud. 'Don't bring Tatum into this Dad. I love her. She's my choice. It was you and

Mum who wanted Rachel. Just because I'm an accountant doesn't mean that I want a quiet mouse of a wife who hangs off my every word...'

'...sounds pretty good to me...when you get to my age...'

'Come on, Dad. Let's keep on the topic, shall we? You'll need to make some tough decisions if you want any kind of lifestyle at all.'

'I'm sorry, son. I don't mean to be ungrateful. This will turn our lives upside down. My decisions will affect the whole family.'

'No, they won't. Only Sara and Lucy are at home now, and they're not children. It's a normal age and time for us all to be leaving home. That's not your problem—you're worried about Mum.'

'I know. So, let's look at options. We'll have to sell the house, pronto. The Gosford office is the most viable, probably should keep that...We could get a place at Berowra and commute, I guess...Although I...I mean, we all, have so many ties here.' James cleared his throat and looked down.

'All I know, Dad, is that you'd be better off giving this to Mum as a done deal. I know you're used to running everything by her, but if there's any room to manoeuvre, she will. You need to discuss things with your marketing guy. It's a new marketplace for limousine hire these days. There's a younger clientele. You'll have to change things up. I'd think about keeping Chatswood. It mightn't have been your biggest earner this year, but it's the most consistent. Dad, this is business—hesitate and you lose everything. Anyway,' Robert said, 'I think it's time for a break. Let's go and get some sandwiches. Margaret is sure to have made a few trays.'

'Oh dear. She'll have to go...'

'As will most of your staff.'

'Sit down or you'll fall down!' shrieked a voice.

'There goes our Lucy,' said Robert, 'probably talking to the dog.'

'Do not tell me what to do in thish house, young lady,' said Angie.

'Mum you're pissed. Did your afternoon sherry turn into ... did you drive like this? Bloody hell, wait 'til Dad...'

'You're a prishy little prude, Lushee Belmore. Your father ish at work trying to ... unbungle ... something ... bishness. I will not be shpoken to like this.'

'You're not looking for more booze are you? You've had enough!'

'What if I am...?'

Lucy stood in front of her mother, arms folded.

'Who's John Collins, Mum?'

'None of your bishness.'

'Well, he must be a relative of some sort—he's been staying with Nan.'

'Heesh a waste of shpace progidal son who broke my daddy's heart. Walked out after sh-ome row and left home for over twenty yearsh. Shtupid argument...Left me, Left everyone...I needed him. He should never have come back again.' said Angie. A rough jerking sob escaped her; she wiped her mascara smeared eyes with the back of her shaking hand. 'Why are you shtanding there? Lu...'

'To stop you...'

'What...? Who d'ya think y'are, Lu?'

'Don't touch that bottle, Angie.' James was furious.

Robert gave a quick goodbye salute and left. He made it his business to avoid the family's emotional dramas. Dad would have to man up and face this; there would be no peacemaker's path to smooth waters this time.

He had his own future to think about. It was with a sense of relief that he gunned the Subaru into life.

Arriving home he fumbled with the keys, then rushed through the door.

'Welcome home, darling,' said Tatum, as she curled her lush body into him. 'How was it, Robbie?'

'Hmm, okay I guess.'

'A man of few words. Mmm, I think I like that...At least I'm getting on well with your mother now. We've been out shopping all week.' Tatum began to peel off her clothes, slowly. This action had the effect of making Robert deaf to her last sentence. 'Did your father see sense, Robbie?'

'He saw a lot more than he expected,' said Robert, holding her close. 'But I'm not going to talk about that with my future wife as soon as I walk through the door.'

'Why, Robbie! Is that a proposal?'

'No. It's a notification for a pending proposal.'

'Hmm, so I have something delicious to wait for?'

'Oh yes. You most certainly do.'

'But Robbie darling, you know I can never wait to unwrap my presents.' Tatum laughed and claimed his lips in a passionate kiss.

Robert went down on one knee.

'Oh, Robert—*now!*'

'Tatum Gregory, will you do me the honour of marrying me?'

'Oh, Robert. So formal, that's what I love about you. Yes! Yes!' Snaking around him sensuously she drew him into the bed, where they made love in the velvet night. They fell asleep tangled in the sheets.

The phone shrilled. Tatum was awake instantly—an early morning call was no new thing with the hours she kept. Robert was too dazed to pick it up so Tatum grabbed it and handed it to him.

'What ... Dad? ... Is there someth...'

'It's your mother.'

Elise

'Who the blazes is that screaming?' asked Elise.

'Our latest arrival. Fell down the stairs,' said Andrew, the Accident & Emergency registered nurse.

'Must be in a lot of pain.'

'She was dead drunk, love. I don't think she's feeling a thing—yet. Pity help us when she does. The family aren't helping—the husband is wearing out the floor. Two sisters; one won't stop yapping and panicking her father, and the younger one is trying to calm them both down—without success I might add. We can't take X-rays in her current state—throwing herself about, so I'm just waiting for the doctor to sedate her. Then he can examine her.'

'Do there seem to be any serious injuries?'

'I wouldn't think so—the way she's thrashing around and abusing everyone. At least when it comes to broken bones, although the left foot looks a bit twisted, so might be a fracture there.'

'She sounds like a real handful.'

'Don't feel too sorry for *her*, love, she's on her way to Surgical, *to you*, when she settles down. And then withdrawal will set in.'

'Oh great. So it gets worse.' Elise covered her ears. 'How many decibels can the human voice reach? And to think I came down here for some peace and quiet in my break. Make sure the doc sedates her well, please Andrew. Just for me?'

'Never mind *you*, Elise. I'll do it for the benefit of the hearing public, but mostly for myself!'

Elise yawned.

'So, what are you doing on nights anyway?' asked Andrew.

'Karyn asked to do a swap.'

'Again? Does that girl ever do her own shifts?'

'Doesn't make much difference. She doesn't do anything when she is there,' said Elise.

'Why don't you girls put in a complaint? She'd know she was alive if I had her here.'

'Easy to say when you're the RN in charge. I'm just an enrolled nurse, remember?'

'Ah, better go. Here's the doc.'

By the time Angie Belmore reached the ward, she was trembling and pale. Gone was the banshee of A & E. Elise settled her into the ward. Angie drifted off to a restless sleep, and Elise had time to read her notes. She was keen to see how much damage the woman had suffered. The bruising alone was impressive.

However, there was very little damage apart from soft tissue contusions. There'd been a dislocated shoulder, but that had been manipulated in A & E by the orthopaedic registrar. She wore a sling to avoid the shoulder slipping out of place again. There were two fractures to the metatarsal bones on her left foot which had been strapped. Angie would be fitted with a walking boot by the physiotherapist the next day.

It seemed alcohol abuse was her biggest hurdle. She would be assessed and receive medication on the ward until she was well enough for transfer to the hospital detox unit. Then she would probably be referred to the Fenmore Clinic, which was an annexe of the hospital. It was the drug and alcohol rehab centre. If she agreed. And that might just be the sticking point.

The same doctor that serviced Fenmore's, also attended the detox unit and the wards. He would see Angie in the morning to manage her withdrawal symptoms. Hopefully she would be ready to admit she had a problem.

Elise had a day off to make up for the night shift. Angie was being sedated, and having limited visitors for 24 hours. So Elise's arrival back to the Surgical ward coincided with the Belmore Family Zoo, as the youngest, Lucy, called them.

Robert was sombre and practical. He seemed overwhelmed by the ward and everyone except his model girlfriend, who carried expensive water bottles in her designer purse. Perhaps it was the new 'food', thought Elise, Tatum was rail thin.

Apparently Sara, the second daughter recently had an emotional crisis. She sat apart from the others, with what seemed to be a boyfriend of sorts. He was definitely besotted. A definite hunk, that one.

Lucy wasn't tall like her sisters and wasn't quite as thin. She came more often than the others, and was more confronting than all of them put together.

She didn't seem to be angry, just on a mission—dishing up 'reality therapy' of her own devising to Angie. Sometimes a young man came with her who appeared to find her vastly amusing. Elise didn't.

'The caterers are here,' Lucy would say whenever the meals arrived.

'Is the housekeeping up to your standards, Angie?' she asked when the cleaners were there. Apparently she had recently taken to calling her mother by her first name. It was amazing what you learned from family conversations when the family thought no-one was paying attention.

There was more.

'Do you need me to bring you one of your $200 bottles of goop?' 'Nan sends her best wishes.' This one seemed to really put Angie's teeth on edge.

Angie spent most of Lucy's visits in wounded silence, which didn't seem to bother Lucy, because she usually had her head in a magazine. 'I'm just trying to see what a $15 magazine has to offer that the others don't.' 'My goodness, I just must have that $15,000 dress—isn't it a bargain. Just my colour. It will go with this $20,000 Luis Vuitton bag. I can't resist.' 'Oh, now this is a *wonderful* human interest story— they must have rescued a Somalian woman and given her a job modelling, even fattened her up a bit. She looks a bit glum though—oh, wait a minute, it's Naomi Campbell.'

Elise wasn't sure why all of these statements wound Angie up, but being the one who usually had to put up with Angie's moods afterwards, she wished Lucy to parts unknown.

'Ooh look, Angie—there's an honesty test in Cleo this month. Let's do it. What fun!'

Angie cried for two hours after that episode, upsetting the old lady in the bed opposite who assumed Angie had received bad news about some dire terminal illness, and kept trying to get out of bed with a broken hip to comfort her.

Elise had to get the Sister to settle the poor old dear.

Then Elise had to listen to a blistering tirade from Angie on the ungrateful Belmore brood (*why did she ever have them*), scorning the ones who didn't come and cursing Lucy for coming.

Elise began to feel she could do with a drink, never mind Angie.

Brad

'Good morning, Angie. I'm Brad and I'll be looking in on you today.'

Angie grabbed her robe, she hadn't even begun to dress, and while she hadn't thought twice at the hospital about being buck naked, she definitely minded in the Fenmore Clinic.

'Oh, darling. Don't worry. I'm gay—camp as a row of tents, but *more importantly* I'm a professional. Anyway, you're supposed to be up, bed made, dressed and down in the dining room in 15 minutes.'

Angie threw the robe on and tied it. 'Do I really have to make my own bed?'

'When did you last make a bed, toots?'

'About ten years ago, about the same time I stopped washing my own hair because the hairdresser did it,' moaned Angie.

'Oh dear, Dorothy is missing Kansas,' said Brad.

Angie smiled weakly. 'You could put it that way.'

'Well, if you want my opinion—and while you're in here you don't have a choice—Kansas was highly overrated. Come on, dearie. I'll make one side while you do the other. We'll let you break the rules this time, but only because you're new and slower with that whopping great boot. But now that you know, you'll just have to get up earlier.'

'Nobody told me I was going to boot camp.'

'Oh, I'm sure that was covered in the brochure.' Brad deftly flicked the sheets and watched Angie's efforts with amazement. 'You really are useless aren't you, dearie? Well we don't have anything as basic as bed-making training, but we do have a wonderful program after breakfast. Taken by yours truly on Replacing Habits. You can't just give something up without finding something better. You can think of it as finding a better Kansas.'

'As long as there are no witches.'

'Angie, Angie, there are *always* witches. Welcome to the real world.'

'The real world sucks.'

But he was gone, whistling as he went along the hall, greeting the other clients.

So, this is rehab, thought Angie. Six bloody long weeks of it. How will I survive? And when I leave, I won't have a home.

Self-pity settled over her like a fog, endless and cloying. She was sure that she'd throw up if she ate one bite. Or swallowed one ounce.

However, when she arrived in the dining room, the aroma of coffee wafted towards her. She was astounded when she saw the food. It might be boot camp for addictions, but it was heaven for food. Seated as far as she could from the other residents, Angie enjoyed a gourmet breakfast.

Lunch was even more sumptuous. After a Waldorf salad, she had a divine Pavlova. She couldn't remember being this hungry. She survived the morning lecture, or program as they preferred to call them, but only just. Everything apart from meals was directed at facing the past and their addictions. There was nowhere to hide.

A shy woman asked if she could join her at the table. What else could she do but demure? Say she'd rather be alone. She hoped the woman wasn't a chatterbox, then when she didn't say a word, Angie found her silence annoying.

However, she was determined to attend the programs and group sessions. There was no point being here unless she made an effort.

And truth be told, she was almost glad to miss out on the dismantling of her home. Margaret would take care of the packing. What would they do without her? Then Angie realised that they would have to cope if they were bankrupt. That was to be avoided at all costs. She had to make it here. She'd hit rock bottom on every level.

She wasn't allowed visitors for the first two weeks, and that was almost a relief too.

What she feared most were the one-on-one sessions with the therapist.

Brad was very attentive. He managed to relate with ease with the clients without showing any annoyance. His patience was surely tried, but he loved the job.

Angie's case fascinated him. She appeared to have spiralled into out of control with her drinking in the last few years, but there was no obvious reason for the change.

There was something there, under the surface. She wouldn't really progress until they could break through the carefully maintained facade. Something had happened sometime. Some time before the dilemmas that she was blaming, something deeper. She wouldn't open up easily, and probably wasn't even aware of what was eating at her yet. Counselling therapy would have to push her buttons to get at the truth.

His client load was light, designed to give him the maximum time with them. He only had six weeks with Angie. Hopefully he'd be able to find some answers to help Angie in her therapy with Dr Dimitri Kostas, the resident psychiatrist. Angie was one patient he didn't want to relapse. She was facing dependency not only with alcohol but also with sleepers—the dreaded Benzodiazepines, otherwise known as 'benzos'.

He wasn't sure six weeks was enough, but there were outpatient follow ups that would continue. It was a tricky combination, but not uncommon. It was crucial to come off alcohol cold turkey, but with the benzos, the dosage must be scaled down to avoid seizures and other complications. It was crucial that she tell the truth about her usage, otherwise the wrong dose would have dire effects, such as withdrawal syndrome.

Reading through her notes, Brad looked for a clue. She had certainly been initially resistant at the hospital, which was par for the course. Thankfully, the nurses had made lengthy notes of her interactions with family members. Someone had to know something—even if it was subconscious. Sometimes the immediate family were too close to see, or know. Addicts were very good at hiding, not just from others, but themselves. That's why omitting blame was so important. The mother had mild dementia, but she might be helpful.

He noticed that there was a brother, John, who visited often even though Angie refused to see him. Apparently he was the only one to act calmly. He and the family had been estranged, but he'd been close to Angie until he left home. The notes reported he'd said the 'falling out' had been with the parents.

'Hmm. I have a feeling in my waters,' he said to Jeremy, another carer.

'That's a dreadful saying,' said Jeremy, 'can't you just say you have a hunch?'

'I have a feeling in my hunch.'

'Arrggh. You do that on purpose. Okay, I'll bite, what's your 'feeling in your waters'?'

'I think the brother might know something about Angie's past. Apparently she's phobic about her hometown of Tenterfield. I think the key to her past is there.'

'But aren't they estranged? You'd have to tread carefully.'

'Yes.'

John Belmore was more than happy to come in. Brad was pleased, that was a good sign. He asked John to bring anything he had on their life in Tenterfield, or to try and remember that time.

'Thanks so much for coming in, John,' said Brad, 'take a seat, will you.'

'I hope I can help. Ange won't see me. I've been in touch with Mum for years, and was reconciled with my father, but Ange seems unable to forgive me.'

'What for, do you think?'

'Leaving, I guess. Hurting Mum and Dad. I was an ass, a young fool.'

'Is it possible that she was hurt by that?'

'Gosh, I guess so. She was only sixteen, hardly more than a kid.'

'Can you remember anything about her from that time?'

'She was very motivated—ambitious even. I was surprised that she didn't pursue a career. She was doing work experience for the local alderman and quite keen on politics. She was doing a office management course at TAFE. She'd done well at school. On the debate team, theatre, you name it.'

'So, something changed. If we could pinpoint...'

'I wish I was more help. She never really confided in me. Well, who tells their big brother anything? I drove her places, she was just about to get her license. I heard she got it first time she sat the test after I left.'

'So, you kept up with what was happening?'

'Yeah, a mate told me how they all were from time to time. I was just too proud to go home and make things right. I thought I was right and no one could tell me any different then.'

'Well, thanks again for coming, John.' Brad rose and extended his hand. John shook it, clearly upset that he hadn't been able to do anything. 'Look, if you think of anything...here's my extension number. Call me anytime.'

'Thanks, I will.' John shook Brad's hand. 'Oh, there's a paper bag from the hospital. I guess it's some of her clothes or cosmetics. They forgot to give it to her husband.'

'Great, I'll hand it on.'

After John left, Brad examined the bag. Nothing was allowed to be given to the clients without being searched. There were a few items of clothing, and a recent newspaper. Brad spread it out on his desk. It was the Tenterfield Tribune. He flipped the first couple of pages over, then stopped suddenly. There was writing with red felt pen. It was over the face of a man. The article was an expose on the recently deceased Mayor, Mark Henderson. The word Angie had written was "RAPIST".

Hardly able to breathe, Brad read the story.

He had found his key.

Melanie

'Take a seat Jim, I'll be with you in a moment,' said Melanie. She wiped a fine sheen of sweat off her brow. She stirred the heat pack in the 'cauldron' as the physios called the large electric heating appliance. What a time for Jenny to have to go to the post office. She'd be glad when Justin was back again. He was so much more organised, but then Jenny was the receptionist and although she was used to filling in for the two physios for smaller tasks, she became flustered easily.

Melanie wasn't sure why Jenny was heating the pack, but the 'cauldron' had been boiling for a while and it wouldn't do to ruin the expensive heat packs.

'Come through, Jim. I think I'll put you on the TENS machine first,' she said.

'Thanks Mel.' He began to peel his shirt off.

'I'll just close the curtain while you do that.' Her voice was tight. Jim had been coming for a few months now. she hated being alone with him. There was something about him. *Maybe he's just in love with himself. His manners are polished, and he's always immaculately groomed, she thought. He just seems to push the boundaries.*

'Right Jim, I'll just attach the electrodes. You know how it works. Tell me when the stimulation is strong enough, but not uncomfortable...'

'Ha ha. I like the way you talk, Melanie...'

'*Electrical* stimulation, Jim,' said Melanie as she turned the current up much higher than usual.

'Yow. Cut that down. That's too much. You like to punish a man do you, Melanie? That your 'thing'? Is that what gets you...'

'You can stop right there. Do not speak to me that way.'

'Oh come on, Melanie. We're friends; I've been coming for months. We're here alone. Just one little kiss, that's all. I wouldn't hurt you.'

A silent client in the next cubicle grasped the rail until his knuckles went white. His hearing heightened to catch the muffled words and his muscles tensed.

There was a rustle of fabric.

A scream.

'Jim, stop! Why, you're not wearing anyth...'

Thwack.

Dave Richards rubbed his knuckles.

Then, he had time to take in the sight of a man with his hand cupped under a bleeding nose, as he lay partly under the exercise bike—as naked as the day he was born. Dave experienced a shock of recognition. It was James Belmore, Clare's brother-in-law.

When James saw Dave he grabbed the tangled sheet with his other hand and ineffectively tried to cover himself. *'You!'*

'Ah, so you recognise me after all these years.' Dave turned to Melanie. 'Are you all right...er...Miss?'

'I didn't know anyone else was here,' said Melanie, 'did Jenny book you in?'

'I guess...The pregnant blonde said you were a physio short, but to come through anyway because I could still have massage and heat treatment.'

'Oh, thank goodness for Jenny,' breathed Melanie. 'And thank goodness for you...um...'.

'Dave...Richards. New client.'

'Excuse me!' said a loud voice. Both Dave and Melanie looked down. Neither of them bothered to do anything for James's bleeding nose, or his lack of apparel. 'Can't you help me here?'

'No!' said Melanie and Dave at the same time, returning to their conversation.

'Is your assistant, ah...Jenny coming back? She looked

very pregnant.'

'Oh, she's carrying the baby at the front. That probably means she's having a boy.'

'Really is that what they say?' said Dave. He was standing in his track pants and singlet and massaging the rubbing liniment onto his right elbow. 'Sorry, I got sick of waiting and helped myself to the liniment bottle.'

'What happened to you?' asked Melanie.

'Tennis elbow.'

'*Excuse me...!*' shouted James.

'Shut up,' said the other two.

'You pair twins or something?' growled James. 'Could whoever is standing on the sheet, get off so I can get up and leave this lousy place.'

'Tennis? You must be playing too much.' Melanie frowned.

'No, it's more a matter of playing for the first time in twenty years...'

'Oh, that would do it...'

'...to impress my daughter, Sara.'

'She must love that—playing with her dad. Must be nice to have a daughter...'

'For God's sake!' yelled James.

'It would have been better if *this bastard down here* hadn't stolen her for nearly twenty years...'

'What the...?' squealed Jenny, the pregnant assistant who walked in to see a naked bleeding man struggling to get up from the floor, and her boss chatting casually to a man with a machine attached to one arm, while he massaged the other.

Not much later, travelling home in the car, James thumped his head on the steering wheel and bellowed. That guy couldn't talk, running off and leaving a pregnant teen.

Not that he knew she was pregnant. James had seen to that. He couldn't believe his luck when Dave came strolling down the quiet farm lane. James thought he'd gone for good.

Dave had genuinely been shocked to learn Clare was only sixteen. James threatened him with jail, told him Clare never wanted to see him again. And then he'd punched the living daylights out of him and walked away. Dave was young and easy prey. So naive—believed Clare was older. That news scared the crap out of him. So much for city smarts. James chuckled.

Everyone in the family thought he had just disappeared. And no-one knew Dave had come back for Clare. No one suspected reserved, polite, good old James of anything.

Damn. 'Good Old James' could come undone. James thought of how to rescue his reputation.

Now Dave had something on him—thanks to today's fiasco, and the timing couldn't be worse. Dave was bound to open his mouth, unless...James agonised over how to manage some damage control. He could handle Angie's life unravelling; she was a drama queen anyway. But not his life—he'd worked too hard.

Oh, blast. What the hell is that? I'm on fire. I'd better drive to the side of the road. I feel as though someone has poured petrol on my crown jewels. My jocks feel hot and slimy...Bloody hell, where's the nearest toilet? I'm going to pass out. What's happening?

Then he remembered that Dave was rubbing liniment on his arm before throwing James his clothes.

That bastard. I'll kill him.

'Oh Jenny, shut the clinic up. Put the illness sign up.'

'Thanks, Melanie. I feel a bit faint—I might lie down on one of the cots. Honestly I leave for five minutes and the place goes to wrack and ruin.'

'So you know that guy, Jim?' asked Melanie, lightly resting her hand on Dave's arm.

'Don't get liniment on you,' said Dave, with a sly smile. 'You know what can happen...Why I think our friend James might be suffering some...minor discomfort...right about now...'

'You didn't!'

'Ah huh.'

'Where?'

Dave rolled his eyes.

'*No!*'

'Oh, yes,' said Dave.

And just because her beautiful brown eyes were wide and she was focused intently on him, he told her the whole story.

Melanie laughed and cried. And hoped that this warm and funny man, with his big open heart might be single.

'Thank you so much, Dave,' Melanie said. She heard Jenny softly snoring in one of the cubicles. 'I was shaking with fear until you rushed out. I thought I was alone. He seemed a bit drunk, but it was the middle of the day.'

'I hope he doesn't come again. Is he a regular client?'

'Not any more. I feel so grubby. He's always seemed a bit in love with himself, but he's never crossed the line. It's offensive to be...to have...someone think you're like that...as if this is a massage parlour instead of a physiotherapy clinic.' Melanie shuddered.

'Well if you ever...ah, you know...need...' said Dave.

'Yes?'

'Well, um...me...I suppose...' said Dave.

'What would I do if I thought...well if I did...um...need you?' asked Melanie.

'Oh, here's my card...you can ring me anytime. Actually I'd like it...You might get...hungry or...'

'I'm a bit hungry now...actually,' said Melanie.

'Good. Yes...we could...you know...if you...'

'Did you stutter as a child?'

'No, but I was terrified of girls.'

'You're not very good at this, are you?'

'Useless. Let's grab a meal before we starve or turn to pillars of salt,' said Dave, happiness shining from his eyes.

'That's the longest invitation for a date in history,' muttered Melanie, 'but quite possibly the sweetest.'

Duncan

'Have you seen my hairbrush?' asked Sara.

'No, but I've found enough hair to cover a mammoth. Are you moulting?'

'I'm not a cat, Duncan. Anyway, I've had my hair cut, thanks for noticing.'

'Oh, I thought something was different. Are you going out? It's getting a bit late, isn't it?'

Sara frowned.

'Okay, I'll stop 'smothering' you. How was work?'

That should be a safe subject, he thought. *It seems to be the one thing she can talk about. It's stupid, we used to talk about everything, and now it's like being with a clam.*

'I love it so much, you know. It's like everything I enjoy combined. I can't wait to finish my arts degree and work there full time. There's this divine table that was in the exhibition. Either Dave or Jamie bought it, I don't know which. And I don't know who it's for, a client.' she sighed.

'You'd like it to be yours?'

'In my dreams. Ellie said it was weird looking, but I'll bet it costs less than a few pairs of her shoes.'

'I'll make spag bol and you tell me about everything.'

'I don't think I want anything heavy this late. I'll have nightmares.'

'Thanks, is that all you can say about my cooking? You want something else?'

'I'll just make a cheese sandwich.' Sara wandered around Duncan's small kitchen in the flat above his garage. 'Thanks so much for having me here, Duncan. I know how old fashioned you are about this kind of situation. You've put up with me for a couple of months now. I only intended to be here for a couple of nights.'

'Where were you going to go?'

'I don't know. I just wanted to get out of home. Then Mum fell, and I feel bad, but I can't go back. Not yet. Anyway, she seems to be doing okay in rehab. I never thought she'd go—not in a million years.'

'Maybe she's lost some of her pride.'

'Yeah, right.' Sara stood looking in the fridge.

Duncan laughed. 'Are you hoping the sandwich will jump out at you? You remind me of Joe. He does that.'

'Your brother never stops eating. No fridge is safe.' Sara laughed. 'Actually, that spag bol smells great. I might have a bit. Will there be enough for Joe?'

'He'll be thrilled that you care. Yes there will, you know I make heaps.'

'Yum, this is delicious.' She yawned. 'Why is it that warm food makes you sleepy?'

Duncan paused. He waved his fork, wondering whether to bring up the subject. 'What are you going to do about your mother, Sara?'

'Which one: the one who lied about my parentage? Or the one who lied about...?'

'I get it. Have you seen either of them?'

'No.'

'I've never seen you like this.'

'I've never *been* like it.' Sara slumped into the chair. 'Oh, Duncan, I'm sorry. I don't mean to take it out on you. I just don't want to see either of them—not yet. It's much easier to be around Dave. We have so much in common, and there is a crucial difference...'

'He didn't lie.'

'Yes, and he insisted on DNA, but I'm glad he did because now I know for sure. The best thing is that he expects nothing from me—no pressure, no guilt trip. Clare could have done something. She spent all those years happily on the sideline, having a nice uncomplicated single life. She didn't put up much of a fight for me. And now, suddenly, it's so important for her to see me and explain. She and Mum both...it's about justification.'

'You're assuming a lot, Sara. You don't know their stories.' Duncan paused. 'Are you sure some of the attraction doesn't come from his Romeo stepson? You've been spending some time with him too.'

'You promised you wouldn't do that, Duncan. I thought we had an understanding. Friends—no jealousy, no rules, no pressure.'

'Sorry.'

'Do you have any idea what Dave's been through? How much he wanted a child? I'm a wonderful surprise to him— a gift he never thought he'd have. A bonus, not a problem to hide or handle.'

Duncan reached out and gave her a quick hug. Sara accepted it warily.

'I hate to see you going through this, Sara.'

She shrugged.

'I guess we'd better get an early night if we're going to help sort and pack the house tomorrow. Dad will need help and I don't want to let Lucy and Robert down.'

'What about letting Ellie down?'

'Huh!' said Sara, 'it's Ellie who lets everyone down. She'll be afraid to break a nail. She'll probably spend all the time talking to Robert's new girlfriend and getting in the way. Then Margaret will end up doing everything as usual.'

'She's quite a women, that Margaret.'

'She's a living doll,' said Sara.

'You feel okay with your Dad? That surprises me. He'd have to at least be as much to blame as the others.'

'You're right, I guess. But he's just 'good old dad'. He seems so disconnected from it all.'

'And that's a good thing? Sheesh, you Australians have weird ideas about family.'

Duncan discovered just how 'weird' the next day.

He came upon Ellie giggling on the phone and blowing kisses. He heard the name she 'whispered'. It was a doctor from the research clinic. He was married with two small children. She hung up. Minutes later, she was all over Brian.

James was in a daze. His nose was swollen and he sported two spectacular black eyes. Duncan was worried how Sara's father would react to him being there, but James seemed relieved Sara had come. He was walking a bit funny too. If Duncan didn't know better, he'd think James had had quite a night. But it didn't pay to be observant in this family.

Robert, who was usually a rock of activity, kept being distracted by Tatum who was in an amorous mood and kept slipping her hands up his shirt and kissing his neck. Usually one to be embarrassed by public affection, Robert surprised everyone by responding passionately until Sara told them to get a room—'*in Western Australia, if possible*'.

Tatum needed more instructions than a pre-schooler, and talked nonstop—everything from 'where is the filtered water' to 'which loo are we using' 'how can anyone wear these gloves, they make you hot' 'hey, everyone—we're engaged—just waiting on the ring YAY!'

'Well, it's not official then,' Ellie said.

'You're just jealous,' said Tatum.

'Ha!' said Ellie. She declared the dust from the books was making her sneeze and had given her a headache that would 'split bricks' and she needed to lie down. While getting the headache pills from her purse she spilled the whole contents on the floor.

Brian went to help her pick everything up and found the contraceptive pill. Then there was a furtive discussion between them, where both thought they were whispering, but weren't. Brian asked why she had The Pill when she was making him wait, *like forever*. Ellie was indignant, declaring they were to regulate her cycle.

She sulked. Then Brian was miserable because he'd upset her. He said 'I'm sorry, Baby' until Lucy told him he was making everybody sorry.

Tatum took Ellie to get a drink of water, muttering slyly,

'Well done you.' Ellie smiled and made a zipping sign across her lips.

When she came back from the kitchen, Brian settled her solicitously on a sofa in the lounge that hadn't been loaded, calling her 'my poor pet', and then did the work of ten men.

Ellie came out after a couple of hours, and gave Brian a condescending pat. Brian smiled from ear to ear. Sara said he was trying too hard with everything, not just Ellie. After a few hours of his silent intensity, manic packing and relentless stacking, Duncan was inclined to agree.

'I don't know why we're doing all this, we have the removalists coming,' said Sara, then realised there would be no paid help this time. She put her head down and packed books, dusting them as she went.

Angie's friend, Sylvia, flew through on a cloud of expensive perfume, bringing a Pavlova and a bottle of champagne. 'Aren't there any other friends here to help, darlings?' she asked, hovering by the door, ready to leave again.

'Friends? What are they?' said Lucy.

'Never mind, darlings. Here's some nourishment from Auntie Sylvia. Enjoy the champers. Too-da-loo!'

Right! So useful, thought Duncan, missing his Mediterranean family. He wondered if perhaps he might be better off with a girl who thought family was supposed to be a close community and not a zoo. Sara hadn't said a word all day.

After a few hours, the champagne bottle was empty and Tatum and Ellie were giggling and promising to be 'BFF, yes, Best Friends Forever, yes forever.' Then they sang the words off key to the tune of *I Will always Love You.*

This started Binty howling, which was rather odd for a Spaniel, before he decided to use the timber staircase as a Stairmaster. Up and down, up and down. His clattering nails on the polished boards caused everyone to tell him to shut up. He had to be put outside. Unlike everyone else, he thought the whole proceedings were exciting.

Lucy went outside to take stock of the outdoor furniture. She came back in crying because all the neighbours were out watching, and someone had asked her if they were going to hold a street stall for the 'stuff that wouldn't fit in the next place'. She'd been unusually quiet all day, so her sobbing shocked them.

James tried to console her by bringing a roll of toilet paper because he couldn't find tissues. Duncan would have been surprised if James could find anything.

Robert and Brian went hell for leather packing the truck. Brian said he was up for the job as he was the fastest in his class with the Rubix Cube. Tatum and Ellie sniggered. Brian didn't seem to notice.

When it came to efficiency, of course it was Margaret who outdid them all. Organisation beat muscle hands down. Duncan heard her on the phone and realised her friends called her Maggie. She obviously also had a PhD in discretion. Duncan saw more vodka bottles slipped quietly into the mini skip bin than at his uncle's restaurant after a footy game. Angie was a genius at hiding things. She would have been great in a POW camp.

Lucy, who had Jamie in tow, followed Margaret around asking for instructions. Duncan realised how well she and Jamie worked together. He'd never seen Lucy quiet and focused, but then he'd never seen her in her natural surroundings.

Sara burst into tears over something Ellie said, and declared she'd had enough of them all and was leaving. Which meant Duncan was leaving.

Thank God.

'I want to see my mother,' she wept in the car.

'Well, I don't think they allow visitors at this...'

'I mean Clare.'

'O k a y.'

The drive up to the Blue Mountains was surprisingly soothing. Sara slept, only wriggling occasionally to change position. The air turned crisp and clear, like the purest of water as they reached the incline before Leura. Sara seemed oblivious, but Duncan drew in the fresh air with delight.

I'm not sure how the reunion of mother and daughter will go when Sara hasn't contacted her first, he thought.

In a Greek family it was the 'norm' but Australians didn't take spontaneous visits quite as well.

'We're here,' said Duncan, stroking Sara's arm.

'Oh good,' said Sara, flying out of the car. She grabbed the key from under the ceramic frog and flew inside. Duncan followed quietly. 'Oh my God! What...'

Clare was entangled with a pair of masculine legs, and only partly covered with a colourful length of fabric that looked straight out of Arabian nights, or the local incense shop.

'Who's this?' The legs had a voice.

'My daughter, Sara.'

'Oh! Come on in. Don't be shy, sweetie,' rumbled the slightly slurred voice.

Sara turned, arms flailing uselessly, and she ran straight into Duncan.

Clare's statement of 'Darling, do let me explain' had no effect on Sara. She was in the car before Clare could gather the fabric around her.

Duncan had a suspicion that Clare often dispensed with such mundane things as clothing when no one was there...or certain someones...

'Where to now?' he muttered.

'Dave's.'

'Right,' said Duncan, feeling as if he was on the television set of some over-the-top non-stop action drama show. As for the 'family meeting' at the rehab centre in the morning— he didn't want to know.

His heart ached for Sara as she cried pitifully all the way down the mountain. But she obviously wanted to face this alone, and that just didn't work for him. If they weren't in the tough times together, they'd never make the good times last. They'd never be able to trust the good feelings, the happy days. Well he wouldn't anyway.

Dr Whitecoat

'You know we are on first name basis here at the centre. Why do you call me Dr Whitecoat, Angie?' asked Dimitri.

'Oh, I don't know,' she said, looking around the office where she'd had daily sessions with Dr Dimitri Kostas. 'You wear a white coat?' She made an attempt at laughing, but it came out as a nervous cackle.

She concentrated on the room. The austerity was broken by a huge window behind the doctor that looked out over the parklike grounds.

'Have you any thoughts on it? Remember there are no right or wrong answers.' Dimitri waited. He was a patient man. 'You like this room, Angie?'

'Oh yes, there's so much light and air. And yet it's also professional.'

'Is those things important to you? Both light and professionalism? Tell me about those two things.'

'I've forgotten how much I enjoyed the country. Ever since I came to the city...well the family came...I've lived a hectic life, so it's a surprise to find I can enjoy a slow pace. I had such ambitions once. I was interested in politics. I had a job—oh well...'

'What happened to your career ambitions?'

'Oh the usual, you know; kids, house, husband.'

'For some women that is enough, but not usually ambitious ones.'

'Hmm,' murmured Angie. The sessions were getting harder. She was exhausted after each one. She'd been here five weeks and the family group session was tomorrow. She was anxious about that and having trouble concentrating.

'What about the 'professional' side?'

'Oh, I guess that's always been important to me. Separation...you know, um, distance in the work place.' Angie knew she was not being very clear, but it didn't seem clear to her either.

'You don't like an informal workplace?'

'No. Take James's office—everyone is casual with everyone else, and there are no boundaries at all. It's 'dear' this, and 'love' that...' Angie shuddered.

'Who is 'everyone'?'

Tears began to trickle down Angie's face.

'Oh, I'm sorry—I'm such a mess, I don't know what I'm feeling half the time.'

'That's okay, Angie. It's actually a good sign.'

Angie gave him a doubtful look.

'You've been using alcohol to numb the bad feelings, but you end up numbing the good feelings too.'

'But I don't have anything to feel bad about. It's...I have a great life...What's that? Oh God...'

Dimitri had placed a newspaper on the desk. It was a Sydney paper and it was a few weeks old. The title read, *'Scandal Surrounding Former Tenterfield Mayor Deepens'*. There was a photo of Mark Henderson.

Angie began to shake and hyperventilate.

Dimitri gave her a drink of water. 'Breathe slowly, Angie. You can do this. You're stronger than you think.'

'Who wrote...that, that word...on there?' Angie pointed to the word 'RAPIST' that was scrawled over the face of Mark Henderson, in what looked like lipstick.

Something stirred within her, something cold and menacing. She began to tremble uncontrollably.

'I think you did, Angie.'

'Me?' Angie's voice was small and far away. Silence wrapped around her like a cocoon. The clock ticked, but neither that, nor the noises of the outside world intruded.

Dimitri waited. Angie must break the spell herself.

'He raped me.' She covered her face with her hands. 'I never thought I could say that.'

'You will be okay.'

'How can I possible ever be okay again?'

'You will. Trust me. Tell me about it.'

'I had just turned seventeen...' The dam wall had burst. Angie recounted that awful night. The night that scarred her, took her innocence and trust. The story she'd never entrusted to anyone. She told of the exhausting efforts she'd taken to hide this 'shameful secret'.

'The shame is not yours, Angie. You did nothing.'

'But, why did he pick me?'

'Because of his own evil desires—nothing to do with you.'

'If I hadn't admired him so much. If I hadn't gotten in to the car that night. I chose those things.'

'And he used them to abuse you. To take from you, against your will. You didn't ask for sex or violence.'

'Why couldn't I tell anyone? That girl, Katie, was so brave. I could never do that. I thought I could forget. Push it down.'

'Most women think that, but it comes back. Quite often when the victim has a daughter the same age, or...' Dimitri said.

'Oh my God that's it. That's when it started to haunt me.

When Ellie was seventeen...that's when the awful nightmares came back. They weren't about him...but I couldn't breathe, there was a weight on top of me and I couldn't move or scream.' Angie shuddered.

'Did you tell James about the nightmares?'

'Just that I was having them...' said Angie.

'And?'

'He said I was neurotic—always had been. Always made mountains out of molehills. Said I was disturbing his sleep. Told me to see a shrink.'

'Did you?'

'No, I saw our GP. He said I had a lot of stress, and gave me sleeping pills.'

'Did they help the nightmares?'

'...No, they didn't, but with sherry...' Angie looked down.

'Did anyone notice your alcohol use?'

'Margaret did.'

'Who's Margaret?' asked Dimitri.

'Our housekeeper, but she's been more like a friend...She was very subtle, she didn't say anything in front of James.'

'What did she do?'

'She just took the glass out of my hand once and said, 'It's no good for using as a painkiller, lassie. I don't like to see you like this', then she just walked away sadly.'

'So she reached out to help you, even risking her job?'

Dimitri said.

'I guess so, but I would never sack her for that...'

'Lots of people would.'

'How awful. I didn't believe her that I had a problem, but I'd never take it out on her. She has a heart of gold,' said Angie.

'And now? Do you believe her now?'

'Yes, and it terrifies me. I'm afraid to go home. It's too soon.'

'A lot of people find the transition hard, but you can come back here as an outpatient.'

'Really, can I?'

'For private sessions, but not for the lectures and activities. You may want to join AA for that.'

'Oh, I'll think about that. Can I see you?'

'Certainly,' he smiled, 'as long as you don't call me Dr Whitecoat.'

'Okay. Thank you, Dimitri.'

'You're welcome, Angie Belmore. Now, get a good night's sleep. We have the family meeting tomorrow.'

'Oh, I'd forgotten. I think those two things are mutually exclusive.'

'There's always the spa. And if all else fails, you can do the homework I gave you, 'Things I can do in my new life'. I'm sure you can come up with something.'

Whether it was the fear of the family meeting and her desperate need not to think about that, Angie did start her list.

To her surprise she found there were things she wanted to do. Even thought of work and career tickled tantalisingly at the corners of her mind. Perhaps she could manage one of their hire outlets.

Seeing things in black and white made her quite optimistic. So even though she had only had a few hours' sleep, she looked forward to the day. She could make a new life. At least the family were coming. That was a good sign. It spelled support of sorts, and she needed all the help she could get.

She smiled brightly as they filed in. Robert pecked her on the cheek. He was followed by Tatum—Angie hadn't expected her. Wasn't this only for family? Her heart sank a little but she pulled herself together. Ellie came in. She was grinning, that was good, but she didn't look at Angie. She sat next to Tatum, and they both promptly got their mobile phones out and began texting. James crept in, adjusting his tie as if it was too tight. He was sporting two rather dramatic black eyes. He sat down with great care.

'Ange,' he said.

Angie was confused. James was acting very odd, as if he was at the courthouse, not at a short counselling session.

Never mind, she thought, men hate counselling. I can't name one of my friends who could talk their husbands into couples counselling.

Lucy came in red-eyed and sad. 'Hello, Mummy,' she said, kissing Angie. 'Sorry for calling you Ange, and...' Angie patted her face.

Iris wasn't there, but Angie was okay with that—pleased even. Her mother had been through enough. They had spoken on the phone, and progress had been made. They were still angry, but they were talking.

Angie had warned Dimitri that Sara might not make it. She'd spoken about the situation to Dimitri at length. So she was really shocked when Sara peeped tentatively into the room, and asked in a calm clear voice, 'Would you be okay if Dave comes, Mum?'

'Ah hmm. I don't think...' said James, but stopped instantly at the look on Sara's face.

'It's up to Mum, James.'

Oh dear, thought Angie.

Angie tried to look around Sara to see if Clare was there, but she could only see Dave.

Things were going downhill. 'Sure, she said. How much worse could things get? She was glad Dimitri had warned her not to be too hopeful. Her family were acting as if she had leprosy, so why not have the family hangers-on too.

Dimitri came in and introduced himself.

Tatum asked if there was a rubbish bin for her used gum.

'Tatum, really,' said Ellie, waving her hand in Tatum's face.

'Oh my God! You have an engagement ring! You did that out of spite. You always have to be one better than me. You were upset that I...'

'That's rubbish,' said Ellie. 'It's coinci...'

'Excuse me, ladies,' said Dimitri.

They sat silently. Tatum tapped her foot loudly. Ellie moved her chair noisily—away from Tatum.

Dimitri asked everyone to introduce themselves. When he learned that Tatum wasn't immediate family he politely asked her to wait outside as this meeting was designed to resolve family issues that related to Angie's recovery.

Tatum was furious. She clattered her handbag onto the coffee table, threw her mobile in, then looked at Robert. 'Well!' she said. Robert looked confused. 'Well, Robert, are you going to stand by your future wife, or stay here and let me be humiliated.' Robert certainly knew what she meant then, and they were gone so quickly everyone was shocked. They could just hear the angry clacking of Tatum's high heels.

'Bitch,' said Ellie.

'Oh heck,' said Lucy.

'Lucy!' said Sara.

'What?'

Here we go again, thought Angie.

James looked longingly at the door. 'How long will this take, I'm not feeling crash hot,' he said.

'Well, you wouldn't be *would you, James,*' said Dave, 'after being punched in the face by a female who didn't want your amorous attentions. You shouldn't have made a pass at a physio, old boy.'

'It was an accident. Yes, it did happen *at* the physio. Don't listen to him. Who is he anyway? Nobody.'

'I can't take anymore. You're all barbarians,' said Ellie as she rose and left.

Angie's optimism died.

'I might be nobody to you, but Melanie and Irene are just outside. They'll straighten this out.'

Everyone looked out the window. Two women were on the bench. Angie recognised James's secretary.

'Irene's just narked that I put her off. Ange, you can't listen to these people.' He paused. 'We're supposed to be here for Ange. Isn't that right, darling.'

'You were on the phone for hours last night to someone, Dad. You said the two of you would run the Gosford office, and leave Chatswood to sink. You laughed quite a bit. Oh my... are you having...? Who was that?' asked Lucy.

'This has nothing to do with Irene...or anyone. This is a farce,' said James. He jumped up to leave. The tall vase of reeds and lilies fell onto his groin. He screamed with pain and sunk into the lounge, writhing. 'I'll get you for this, Richards.'

'What, the same way you thrashed the daylights out of me when I came back to see Clare?'

'James...you didn't! Dave came back? How could you? Oh good grief, it all fits,' said Angie.

'You have no idea how hard it's been to live with you, Ange. You're a complete whack job.'

Angie picked up some magazines and threw them at him. She paused. 'Leave now, James.'

Lucy and Sara burst into tears.

'Oh darlings, I'm sorry, please stay?' Angie looked at Dimitri for confirmation.

He smiled. 'Of course they may stay if they want.'

Both girls nodded vigorously.

Dave patted Sara, 'I'll wait in the car, pet. Okay?'

'And then there were three,' muttered Angie. 'Sorry Dimitri. We were supposed to sort out a support team.'

'Ah, but we have, Angie. We have.'

sylvia

'James? My goodness darling, you look dreadful. What shocking bruises,' said Sylvia, opening the elegant French doors, letting in the crisp night air. 'I wouldn't have known you. What on earth happened?'

'Oh, Sylvia sweetheart, you wouldn't believe the day...well the week...I've had.'

'But you were only going to the family meeting at rehab. Did Angie do this?'

James hesitated. He would have loved to pin that on Angie. Any other time he might have gotten away with it, but too many people had been there. Tatum was one of her models and would be only too happy to dish the dirt on him to her boss.

The fact that Angie was the one who reacted the least, irked him no end. His hope that she would come out as the nutcase alcoholic, and he as the longsuffering husband, was also dented by Dave's presence. Especially as he'd arrived with Sara, and opened a can of worms by letting everyone know what really happened all those years ago. He would have bet a king's ransom he would never lay eyes on Dave Richards again. How wrong could he be?

'No. Can't you just take pity on a guy and not give him the third degree?' James snaked his arm around her. 'You know what I've been through with that neurotic witch. I was hoping to stay the night. We've had so few chances to be together all night.'

Sylvia returned the kiss he offered. 'So we're finally going to be together are we? Mmm, I can handle that, my sweet. You told Angie then?'

'I didn't get a chance to say anything at the meeting. That was days ago, and now I get legal papers for a separation. Property, the lot.'

'Well, isn't that what you wanted? What we've been waiting for?' Sylvia stepped back and wrapped her silk robe around her.

'Of course. But not until I've had a chance to sort the business out.'

'What do you mean, James? What is there to sort? I thought you were on solid ground.'

'So did I. But limousine hire is a luxury commodity now.

With the GFC...'

'You told me you were fine.' Sylvia sat on the single lounge chair, forcing James to sit opposite her. 'The news headline would read 'Belmore Limousine Hire Romps through Financial Crisis'. Isn't that what you told me?'

'Can't we just go to bed? I'm zonked out. I don't think I can take any more pressure.'

'Now, you're beginning to sound neurotic.'

'Well thanks, Sylvia. I thought I could count on you.' James sat back and rubbed his temples.

Sylvia noticed that his blonde hair was greying. She'd been attracted to his Adonis good looks. Tall, charming and ... well rich. The whole package. A package that was looking decidedly frayed around the edges. Usually she would have jumped into bed without a thought. Be careful what you wish for, she thought. An astute business woman herself, Sylvia wasn't about to let go until she found out what they were facing. She intended a new life with this man.

James sighed. His fling with Irene hadn't been this much trouble, he thought. Irene had hung off his every word and waited on him hand and foot. Perhaps the reason he'd become bored with her.

Sylvia knew her power over him. She exuded exotic romance, independence, and knew how to use it. It was an irresistible recipe to men, and had helped her career enormously. A former model, she was slim and toned, but also curvaceous heaven with class and style to burn. James couldn't get enough of her. He wanted her now, but she wasn't going to make it easy. But then, she never did. It was part of her attraction. She would not be owned.

Never married, she knew what she wanted and how to get it. For her to want him, gave him a feeling of power, but this time she was playing hard ball.

For the first time in their two year relationship, James had doubts. Would she wait for him? Was she ready to settle down? She wanted answers.

'I can't afford a divorce now. I need to make Angie to drop this nonsense.'

'You need...'

'She owns most of the business.'

'What does 'most' mean?' asked Sylvia.

'50%, but...'

'But what...?'

'Her mother owns 10%. Before all this I could count on Iris to be on my side...' His shoulders slumped. 'I can't believe I've been through months of hell and we have a chance to be together for a few nights, and you're grilling me about business. I don't ask you about yours. I thought our relationship transcended money.'

'I'm sorry, James. Of course, money doesn't matter—I

love you any way at all. I just don't want you to ever lie to me. This is about the truth, don't you see?' Sylvia rose from the chair and pulled James to his feet. As he leaned in to kiss her, her robe slipped open.

'That's more like it,' he said.

Sylvia sighed. She hoped her quick capitulation wouldn't make James suspicious and ask about her finances. Just in case he wanted to delve into the subject, she kissed him with passion. James reached for her, losing himself in her embrace.

After James was asleep, Sylvia mused over her dilemma. There must be another way to find out what she wanted to know. Tatum was engaged to James' son, and the girl would sell her own grandmother for a designer wedding dress. Luckily, Sylvia knew just how to arrange the perfect dress without paying a cent, not that Tatum would need to know that minor detail.

A bridal photo shoot should whet Tatum's appetite. But how to broach the subject? Tatum was nobody's fool. In the end it proved easier than she thought.

'I hear the in-laws aren't entirely thrilled with you and Robert?' said Sylvia, when she was running over the details of the fashion shoot.

'That's an understatement,' said Tatum, 'Angie wanted sappy Rachel, the 'girl next door' and James liked her because her parents are wealthy. But the way those two are carrying on...I thought I was making headway with Angie but that's all undone.'

'How are their finances? I heard...oh never mind...'

'Gosh, I never thought of that...Robert does their business finances. He was over there one night for ages. The night Angie came undone...you know. He talked everything over with his father.'

'Oh, so he's in the know about it all, then?'

'Hmm, the lot basically. Tax, projected outcomes, shares. Keeps their papers at home.'

'Really? Not at work?'

'No.' Tatum was deep in thought. 'Family stuff, you know...'

Sylvia's mind was twisting and turning. She'd put the question in Tatum's head. Tatum would be dying to look. All she had to do was find a way to get Tatum to share the information. That wasn't going to be easy without giving her own motive away, but Sylvia was a patient woman. She shrugged an elegant shoulder. Time was on her side.

Wearing a pencil thin skirt and an exquisitely embroidered teal blouse, Sylvia was at her desk in the model agency early, as usual. She went over the details of the bridal shoot with the girls.

'Have you a minute, Tatum?' she asked.

'Sure, Sylvia. I'm so excited to be doing a bridal shoot,' said Tatum. 'Any chance on a discount? I might be needing one soon.'

'You know the designers don't...' Sylvia murmured, pretending interest in the paperwork.

'Ah, I know. A girl can dream.'

'Although this designer does owe me a favour...' Sylvia tapped the brochure in front of her.

Tatum gasped. 'Oh, my. What would it take?' she asked, eyes sharp.

'Photocopies of what we just talked about, and no questions.'

'Done.'

'Excellent.'

'Any dress I choose?'

'Any.'

'Total secrecy...' Sylvia took her glasses off and eyed Tatum. 'I need to be able to trust you, Tatum.'

'Done.'

Sylvia sighed. She was pretty sure Tatum thought Sylvia wanted the information to protect Angie, her best friend. A momentary twinge of guilt nagged at Sylvia. But it wasn't her fault if Angie couldn't keep her husband interested. No one had poured alcohol down her neck. She was nothing but a neurotic drunk. It was hardly even a competition.

Sylvia had waited patiently for James, and soon she would have him. With or without a fortune.

Which was just as well...

John

John ground his teeth. A huge woman was leaning on her shopping trolley in front of the fridge section. Her eyes were dull and she looked like she had no intention of moving for the next century. How did women stand grocery shopping every week?

He reached in front of the woman, and still she didn't even flinch. Maybe she was unconscious. He sent a silent prayer of gratitude for Zoe. How she managed to do this with three boys was beyond him. Since retiring from the Navy he was learning a great many things she did that he hadn't properly appreciated.

She deserved one hell of a homecoming. If only she'd hurry up and join him. Broome was too far away. He missed her more than any of the times he'd been at sea. But then he'd been busy 'doing' something, and not trying to work his way through the emotional minefield that his original family had become.

Oh great. Now there were five geriatrics all having a jolly time in the bread aisle. Chortling and laughing as if they'd just won a bowls tournament. He waited, thinking of how long it would take to go right around. It was a long aisle. Blow it. He nudged the trolley of the man nearest to him.

'Sorry, mate.'

'No, worries.' John moved on with the trolley, struggling with its tendency to stray to the left. Jeez, you'd never have poor upkeep like that in the Navy. What rubbish. After a career of keeping the machinery in pristine working order, it was hard to tolerate this piece of junk.

'Cut that out, Jack,' growled a large female of indeterminate age. Obviously the kid's grandmother. She was holding 'Jack' up by a well-muscled arm. Impressive, thought John, she'd put his boot camp sergeant in the shade. An older boy stood there, rigid with fear of the old woman. But not Jack, he was squirming and calling out, 'Put me down, Gran.' Gran did. The kid hit the floor with a thump.

This place was a zoo. He'd forgotten everything he was supposed to find—just as well Zoe had emailed him a list. Super-efficient Zoe. A bloody long list it was too. Enough for his whole unit. He'd hate to miss anything, he wanted the house set up for the family. He'd cook their favourite creamy moussaka. It was a combination of Zoe's love of the French cuisine of her homeland and John's 'meat meat Aussie throw 'er in mate' cooking. He had laughed 'til tears ran down his face the first time Zoe called his food that—he'd fallen hard and heavy for her.

Pulling out the list, he realised he'd left his glasses in the car. He reached out his arm and connected with something.

'Oww!' wailed a small child, 'that man hit me, Mummy!'

The young mother took one look at John's bulk and hurried away.

When he finally arrived at a checkout with a quick checkout girl and only one customer, he realised the woman who'd been leaning dolefully on the trolley was the customer in front of him. Her trolley was now overflowing. John was gobsmacked. How had she managed that? She was still in the same sad pose, leaning on the trolley, eyes down.

'How are you today, sir?' chirped the checkout girl.

'I'm terrific,' he lied, 'and how are you?'

He didn't know if this was checkout protocol, but he felt sorry for the girl whose day was filled with depressed housewives, cranky grandmothers and unruly children. He was rewarded by seeing the young girl's face light up.

He loaded the car and was ready to take off, only to have a lump of a man with a huge trolley just standing in front of John's car, waiting for his wife to open the boot two cars up.

John inched the car forward and the Neanderthal moved a few inches. Great. John revved past him, hardly caring if he grazed the inconsiderate jerk.

Then he encountered three cars, all stopped near the entrance/exit. The drivers all looked confused. No one moved. Apparently road rules changed as soon as one entered a car park. John hit the accelerator and went round them all, flying out on to the road that was thankfully empty. Empty of cars, empty of human life. Empty of stupidity.

It was a relief to glide into the driveway. He flipped the boot up and carried a load to the front door. The guy across the road with the permanent grin was smiling even wider than usual. He had what looked like a miniature lawn mower.

The guy settled it near the lawn, then appeared to have second thoughts. He moved the thing back to the front of the garage and cleaned it thoroughly. Then he took it back to the lawn and revved it onto life. With meticulous attention he moved it along the edge of the driveway, grass and soil flying everywhere.

John moaned. That's what *he* would turn into—a suburban nutcase. After a life of military precision he could now look forward to pedantic use of household appliances and lawn gadgets.

He had to get a job.

After he put his groceries away, he went to the granny flat at the back to deliver Iris's to her.

'Hi Mum, how's it going?'

'I don't know where anything is...'

'You've just moved in. You haven't had time to unpack yet.'

'Maybe they were right about the schizophrenia...there's something wrong with my head.'

'Mum, don't be daft. You're just a bit forgetful. The specialist knows better than that quack that passes for a GP at the retirement village. You don't have any mental disorder. You kept getting...um ...'

'Urinary tract infections. You're worse than me. Who would have thought they can fuddle your mind. Although, at my age anything can fuddle it. At least knowing I have diabetes and getting the right treatment has helped that.'

'I brought your groceries,' said John, hoping to distract her from the discussion of her ailments. 'Let me help you put them away, and then you can make me a sandwich.'

'When does Zoe arrive?'

'Two days. It's killing me. She keeps teasing me that it might take longer.'

'She has your measure then. A good thing for a successful marriage.'

'My success in marriage is down to two things. I waited

until I was forty, thus over any nonsense, and I married a woman who pays no attention to what I say.'

Iris laughed. 'If that's your idea of pearls of wisdom, it falls a little short. I can't wait to meet my grandsons and my daughter-in-law.'

Iris opened the drawer to take out the photo of John and his family.

'While you stare at that, I'll put your food away. But don't blame me if you can't find anything.'

'It won't matter; I'll be back in my unit with Maggie when her three months leave is up. I'm so pleased something has worked out. Having Maggie as a live-in companion has been a boon for both of us. Maggie was going to have to sell her unit in Pennant Hills after losing her job with James and Angie. Now she'll rent it out and live with me. They were desperate to keep her on, but Angie will have to learn to do things for herself. It's a hard lesson.'

'She's facing a tough time all right.'

'My word, John. You sound almost sympathetic. I've only ever heard you call her a royal pain or a spoilt brat.'

'Maybe there's more to it than that. How can I gloat when she's suffering enough already?'

'Do you know anything that I don't, John? You would tell me, wouldn't you?'

'I wish I knew. And yes, Mum, I'd tell you.'

'You wouldn't try to hide anything because you're worried about my health? I'd find it hard to take, to be kept in the dark. I know I've done my share of covering up, but I'm done with it. She's still my little girl. Always will be.' Tears ran freely down Iris's cheeks. John took her in his arms.

'We can only hope she comes through this stronger,' he said. 'Have a nap, Mum. I have to go and meet someone in town.'

'I'll be all right, son. You go and don't worry about me.'

'I'll always worry about you, Mum.'

'You're a good son.'

'I'm so sorry for the wasted years, Mum...'

'Hush son, life's too short. You're here now.'

John felt a stab of guilt. He was meeting his father, Arthur Walker.

He knew Arthur would want to see his mother, but he wanted to protect her for now. He wouldn't say anything until Arthur broached the subject.

However, the first thing Arthur did when they met was to hand John a newspaper.

John's heart sank when he saw the headline *Mayor Commits Suicide over Sex Scandal*. Arthur's eyes were clouded. John hoped against hope that his father didn't know his role as the mystery rescuer. If it had been necessary he would have come forward, but there was no point if he didn't have to. If he'd learned one thing in life—if you wanted a secret kept, the only way to do it was tell no one.

As casually as he could, John took the paper and read:

'Ms Kate Morris, the original complainant in the Mark Henderson sex scandal stands by her claim that the Mayor raped her when she was working for him on work experience. Rumours abound about Henderson's life and indiscretions, but his wife, Millicent, who is younger than him by 15 years, is standing by her man. Henderson was admitted to the Sandville Public Hospital with rope burns to the neck, but later died when brain activity was undetectable.

'Henderson leaves a grieving wife, four daughters and a confused public. When asked in court last year about the incident, Morris claims that a large man intervened and fought Henderson, injuring him. She was unable to identify her rescuer, claimed Morris, due to the dark night and the shock of the event. The locals are calling the unknown man *The Scarlet Pimpernel*. The mystery man has not come forward, but prosecutors say that will not impede Ms Morris from receiving victim compensation for the alleged assault.

'However, the other women won't see justice. Mrs Clemens, the wife of the Ingleford Real Estate owner, has stated Henderson forced his attentions on her when she worked for the council as a secretarial temp. She claimed it was 'common knowledge' that Henderson liked them (the girls) young'. 'It was just a matter of time,' said Clemens, 'this has been a long time coming, but we will have closure now. We've been heard.'

'Henderson was buried in a private funeral with family only on an undisclosed date and time. Mrs Millie Henderson is said to be taking things very hard according to a close family friend.

'The exclusive story of Ms Henderson's breakdown at the graveside is covered on Page 4.'

'This paper is years old, Dad. Why do you have it?'

'There's been more come out recently...oh, you know, the usual. Corruption, council bribes, jobs for the boys, that sort of thing. The whole sordid tale had just hit the Sydney papers. Came out weeks ago.'

'You're not affected in any way are you?'

Arthur sat anxiously. 'I was there you know...'

'What! What do you mean—there?'

'At the grave when they hounded that poor wife.'

'Oh...' John sighed with relief.

'It's worrying me.'

'What? The way the journos treated her?'

'No, well that did bother me, but there's something else niggling at the back of my head.'

'What is it, Arthur?'

'Your sister...what's her name...Angie? The tall blonde one...well, she worked in his office in...oh I don't know what year, but she was still at school. Did work experience...She was a bright spark...'

'Yes, I remember that—feisty as all get out,' said John.

'Well, she dropped out of school suddenly. Never could fathom it.'

John's heart constricted. Suddenly he could fathom a lot of things.

'That would have been soon after I left...'

'Hmm, yeah, I think you have the right of it there, John.'

No, thought John. I've had the wrong of it for a very long time. But I might have things clear now, or I will soon.

Iris

'Mum,' called John. 'Arthur's on the phone.'

Iris jumped. It had been over 20 years since she had seen, or spoken to Arthur Walker. Her heart thudded and her head buzzed. She wasn't sure how to react. So much was going on. Angie had been in rehab for weeks, and Iris was anxious to visit her.

She nodded. She might as well take the call; it was inevitable with Arthur in John's life that she would have to see him eventually. If only she knew what to feel, or think.

Taking the phone John held towards her she answered. Arthur's voice sounded strange. So different from the boy she once knew. Hearing him didn't clear anything for her. She simply didn't know him anymore. It was a lifetime ago.

She agreed to see him. He was in Sydney and it was quite a trip back to Tenterfield. She might as well face him. She told him to come straight over.

'He's on his way over, John,' she said, 'you can stop pretending you're not listening.'

'You're my mother, I worry about you. You've been very ill, old girl. Off with the pixies. You must let me take care of you. At least until Maggie is sorted and moved into the unit with you.'

'Okay, John.' She saluted.

'You'll go on cleanup duty, private.'

'You would truly be disappointed with the results.'

'Hmm. You're probably right. I'll just be out in the shed if you need me. Will you be okay?'

'I'm fine!'

'You *weren't*. I'll never forget you lying there when I walked into your room at the retirement village. Those people should be shot. You wouldn't do that to a dog. They should have done thorough medical tests.'

'As long as you stop blaming Angie for it—she couldn't know.'

'Easier said than done. Look, I'm trying, okay. I'm beginning to have some idea of what life's been like for her.'

'Good. Don't be too ready to judge, JC. You were MIA for a long time.' She wagged a finger at him.

This time *he* saluted. 'JC, bah, unfortunate initials those. Give me no end of grief.'

'Tosh,' she said, waving him away.

When Arthur arrived she was sitting in the farthest corner of the lounge room. It took a great deal of effort to appear composed.

'Come in, Arthur,' she said, rising to greet him.

'Iris, how wonderful to see you.' he handed her a glorious bunch of colourful dahlias. He leaned in to kiss her, but she turned and looked for a vase. She needed time to think. She remembered that he'd been a fast mover.

Arthur sat in the love seat.

Iris sat in the long lounge.

He moved next to her. 'Bit hard of hearing, you know.' He murmured about lost chances, of hardship when he went overseas, the pain of being away from her. 'I was trying to save up enough for us to have a life.' He leaned closer.

'Really, Arthur. You did all that at eighteen—that's admirable.'

Arthur's brow furrowed. He looked confused. 'Well, young love is overwhelming. Time apart is such...suffering.'

'That doesn't exactly explain why you never contacted me. Silence doesn't speak towards passion.'

'Oh Iris, don't hold bitterness over past grievances. We have the chance for a completely new start. Just the two of us.'

'Plus your daughter, three grandchildren, my three kids

and...' She paused, counting on her fingers. '... um...seven grandchildren—all of whom give every appearance of procreating in the near future.

'But Iris...'

It was the moment she'd dreamt of for so many years. She had fantasised about this very situation. What he would say. What she would say. And now that it was here, all she could think of was that she should have gone to the loo before he came.

'It's not going to happen, Arthur,' she said, practising her bladder exercises. 'Our chance was lost a long time ago.'

Arthur seemed to take forever with goodbyes. Finally, Iris bolted for the bathroom.

John held his stomach and laughed uncontrollably when he came inside to check on her.

'It's not funny, son.'

'No? It's hysterical. If his company is this uninspiring for a short time—I can't see 'A Grand Passion' happening anytime in the future.' John lay on the carpet and adopted a falsetto 'Julia Robert's voice', 'I nearly peed my pants,' he warbled, adding gestures from the movie *Pretty Woman*.

Iris laughed, 'Now *that* is funny.'

'Ah, Mum. You make life interesting.'

'I just hope he realises I mean it. He's persistent.' She looked at John sharply. 'His ideas should be discouraged.'

'Oh, *no-no-no*. I'm not getting in the middle of your romantic entanglements. Uh ah. No way.'

'Disentanglements would be the more correct term,' muttered Iris.

'That's not a word.'

''Tis too.'

'Rubbish. I'll look it up in the Scrabble dictionary.'

'You do that!' she called out as he wandered off to find a dictionary.

Iris was fairly sure there wasn't one in John's house. She didn't think he'd spent much time playing Scrabble since he left home at twenty.

She smiled. There were so many memories of happy times. All of them together. It hadn't happened since. Her one prayer was that the family would find some common ground, and put aside their differences.

John's search was interrupted by the doorbell.

'There's a Mrs Maureen Everingham to see you Mum. Do you know her?'

'Oh yes, she's Ralph's sister. I'd love to see her.'

'Well, I'm off to collect Zoe and the boys from the airport; I'll be back in a few hours.' John bent and kissed Iris, then ushered Maureen inside. 'Oh, you brought food, Maureen, you will be popular.'

'It's just fruit and cheese. I heard that Iris has diabetes.'

'Bye, son. I can make a cup of tea for us,' said Iris. 'Welcome Maureen, it's so good to see you. It's been too long.' Iris reached out her arms. Maureen walked warmly into the embrace.

'It certainly has been, Iris, too long indeed.'

'Sit down, dear sister. Take the load off your feet. How are you?'

'Oh, I'm fine for an old duck. You know what it's like when the wheels fall off and your motor jolts.'

Iris laughed. 'I certainly do. I had a recent scare—thought I'd lost my marbles, but I'm improving. At least I remember where I live now.'

'Oh dear, was it that bad, old girl? Or are you taking the mickey?'

'A bit of both really. Now, how did you know I have diabetes? And don't tell me that old chestnut that a little bird told you.'

'Your son, John. I must say love, it's taken me a while to hunt you down.'

'That's a long story. One I couldn't bear to retell.'

'It does get tedious having to go over things.'

'Yes, it requires one to recall, not just retell.'

'Oh Iris, you're such a scream. I remember the fun times we had together.' Maureen took Iris's hand. 'I'm so sorry I let us drift apart. Well, that's not right really. I let you and

Ralph down. We were just so shocked to learn that he was...homosexual. We were angry for you as well...you know...that you were being cheated somehow.'

'Ralph never cheated me of anything, Maureen. I always knew. Right from the beginning. We were best friends at school. We protected each other. He couldn't 'come out' in those days. And we always loved each other as the closest of friends.'

'That is so generous of you...I didn't know...You married so young...I hear many men are confused, marry and then...'

'It wasn't like that. Ralph always was so self-assured. He didn't want to tell your father, he knew the ramifications. George was an inflexible, unforgiving man.'

'He thought he was being Christian.'

'I won't even respond to that. It would make me very angry.'

'How can you be so forgiving? It must have hurt somehow to have a child...then...'

'I fell pregnant at sixteen to a shopkeeper's son. Arthur left to work on the oil rigs before he even knew. Ralph offered to marry me and be a father to another man's child. He loved John, as if he was his own. Ralph was the one with grace. My life would have been so different without him. My family were devout and would have insisted on adoption. Even then, I would have been shunned all my life. That's the kind of family I had. Ralph gave me a true family. Not the usual type, but a wonderful one, just the same.'

'Oh my goodness, we knew none of this.'

'With all respect, Maureen, none of you wanted to know. Ralph was gay—dead to the family, forever.'

'Oh God...' Maureen sobbed.

'So you see it's really me you should look down on, not Ralph.'

'I can't change the past, Iris. But I hope I can change your future.'

Iris was silent.

Maureen pulled an envelope out of her purse. And handed it to Iris. It was a cheque for $397,000.

Iris pulled back. 'What is this, Maureen?'

'We buried George six months ago. I can't say anything except he was stubborn to the end. But the four of us felt you and Ralph had been wronged. We saw how you cared for him, especially after the stroke. We knew you loved him, and he deserved better from us. Times have changed and we've learned. Eric's son is gay. He has vowed to do things differently. He's not going to lose a son through intolerance.'

'So, George didn't leave Ralph anything, but his brother and sisters divided it four ways?'

'Yes, that's the size of it.'

It was Iris's turn for tears. The women hugged.

After Maureen left, Iris put the cheque in her bottom drawer. She would need to think about this. Work out what to do with the money, get used to the idea, before acting on it or telling anyone.

John and Zoe arrived with the three boys. It took little effort then to forget the money with a houseful of noise and activity.

'I'm Shaun.'

'I'm Bwan-non.'

'He's Brandon,' said Shaun, shaking his head.

'I Dewamy.'

'He's Jeremy,' said Shaun, 'they can't talk proper yet.'

'Neider tan you,' said Brandon.

'Can too.'

'Daddee he picken on mine,' said Brandon.

'Mine too,' said Jeremy.

'What's dat fing on the mandle police?' asked Brandon.

Iris froze. She looked up. Oh dear. It was the urn with Ralph's ashes. She hadn't thought. It was a long time since she'd been around little ones. She must put the urn away. Perhaps it was time to let go.

'Outside boys!' said John, in his best deep rumbling navy voice.

Iris wouldn't have been surprised if the tots saluted. She smiled; she hadn't seen her son as a father. Her new daughter-in-law was open, natural, and instantly warm. The three boys didn't faze her.

She was definitely a good match for John. And she had taken being a navy wife in her stride—which can't have been easy. Her English was flawless. The lilt of a French accent was there but it only added to her charm.

Iris was overwhelmed. She had acquired three more grandchildren, each of them more active than the other four put together. But they were all so adorable and outspoken.

'Bonjour, Maman,' said Zoe, kissing both of Iris's cheeks. 'You have made a very good husband for me. I think I love you just for that, but I feel also we will be good friends, non?'

'Certainement,' said Iris, glowing.

'Ah, wonderful. Tu parle Français?'

'I'm about out with that bit,' laughed Iris. 'High school French classes a century ago, you know.'

Zoe laughed.

'Well, merci beaucoup for welcoming me in my own language. You are a thoughtful woman. Now if you will excuse me, I will go and check my cupboards. Come sit with me at the bench? We can become better acquainted.

'Shall I tell you how we met?' Zoe turned twinkling eyes on Iris. 'John is outside with the boys, so he will not interrupt my story with his own mixed-up version.'

'I can't think of anything I'd like better.'

'John was on holiday in Dubai. He did not like it there, but his father had worked there on the oil...you know? It is paradise for some—Artur, he loved it. Some men can make their fortune there.'

Iris made a noncommittal sound. Arthur hadn't told her anything about that. He'd made it sound like he worked for low wages in bad conditions.

'John was a bit tired of the usual tourist places, so he booked a tour for the backblocks of Dubai—the poorer areas. I was translator for the tour guide. I had a six month contract from my company in London.'

Zoe was an interesting storyteller. While she talked, the kitchen utensils flew as she chopped and prepared the food.

'Often we had...you know...ah, "rough necks" I think you say here. Young men who thought they were tough and wanted to see under the belly of life there.'

'Underbelly.' Iris was spellbound. She would never get such insights from her son. Men!

'One day three of these awful men cornered me. John sent them how you say—ah yes, "packing". I was pulled out of the contract and requested to return to the UK.'

'So, he's a hero.'

'Well, you've seen those muscles, have you not? He tells people they came from carrying bags of potatoes.' Zoe laughed. 'I like humility in a man, don't you?'

Iris didn't think she'd ever had a conversation where she'd been asked so many questions. She decided it would take some getting used to. 'I do, my Ralph was a sweet humble man.'

'Yes, John speaks of him with great regard. Thankfully he made his peace with his father—to scorn a parent for being gay—it is unimaginable. All the years John missed with a good man. Ah, never look back...'

'So you went on a date to thank John and things went from there?' asked Iris, thinking it was time she asked a question.

'Oh, no,' laughed Zoe. 'He came back to London with me. We spent the rest of my contract time and his long service wandering Scotland together. Your son knows what he wants. He did not waste the time.'

'And Dubai?'

'Bah, we did not care for the place. John wanted to visit some of the sights Artur told him about, but he had no time for them. John does not like the high life or noisy night life. That's when I knew he'd make a good husband. So many women spend their lives waiting for men to get things out of their system, but they never do.

'Of course, Artur had to grow up after his daughter was born and when Shirley got breast cancer. Artur is been involved in research survey for relatives of long term sufferers. Shirley battled for over twenty years. After two remissions she decided 'no more chemo'. I can't blame her.

'Oh sorry, listen to me ramble on. Artur would have already told you all this when he came to see you.'

'Not exactly *all*,' said Iris. 'Anyway, your romance with John is more interesting.'

'It was not so spectacular—not like celebrity romances. But I would hate that. Who knows where the fake stops, and the real starts? Not for me.'

Tea was a lively affair, and very messy. With three small boys who were tired from travel and play, it was a while before they settled.

Then Iris could retire to her granny flat and wonder how Angie was getting on. Now that her mind was clearer, she was worried. She couldn't remember much of the last year, but she was pretty sure she'd given Angie merry hell at times.

It didn't bear thinking about.

Ralph

They scattered Ralph's ashes at dawn, while the vermillion night gave way to the pink haze of a new day. The gathered on the old jetty where they had all spent summer holidays.

Some sat; some leaned on the aged timber structure. They cried and they laughed. They remembered. They were flawed and life was complex. But they were there.

Lucy read.

"We all see the world through our own distorted gaze. What we remember, what we forget, makes up our life history according to us.

doves fall

peace dies

brittle hearts

cold stone

buried guilt

false shame

muted innocence

muffled voice

cruel burden

harsh crime

soft tears

wrenched choice

crossed purposes

twisted lines

subtle whisper

sharp intent

listen now

light flickers

joy flutters

hope shines

divine comes

From those who have loved you—goodbye, Ralph William
Collins. You are free.

You fought a good fight, you ran a good race.

Forever you will be in heaven's embrace."

They lingered. Until the chill of the evening sent them to their cars with reluctant footsteps. Silent hugs were shared.

confetti

'*Lucy!*'

'What?'

'The veils are over here,' called Ellie. 'What are you daydreaming about? There are some gorgeous little ones. Come!'

'I've found something blue. Is there something old?'

'Apparently Nan has a surprise for that. I don't know about it—ask Sara.'

'Sara!'

'Shush Lucy. We're in a bridal shop. A top end one at that. We'll never hear the end of it from Sylvia if we ruin her "connections",' said Sara.

'I don't know why we accepted her offer of help anyway,' said Ellie. 'She's a home wrecker.'

'And this from the one who supported them all the way. Honestly Ellie, sometimes I think you enjoy being opposite. Dad and Sylvia are living together. Move on,' said Lucy.

'That's rich coming from the sanctimonious one in the family,' muttered Ellie.

'Girls, really,' said Angie, looking at her three daughters with their wide grins and wondered how their careless banter must sound to passersby.

'It reminds me of the times they played fairies in the bottom garden,' said Clare. 'Do you remember the tears and hullaballoo when Robert tore the bottom of Ellie's tutu?'

'Oh yes,' said Angie, 'all three girls cried as loudly as the other. I still have some of those things in boxes.'

'There would be a marvellous piece for 'something old' there. Perhaps not 'old' enough, though.'

'I don't think anything there would satisfy the girls' criteria. Iris is providing that—a river pearl necklace.'

'Oh, that will be lovely,' said Clare .

She was so grateful she'd found a place of comfort in the new family jigsaw. Sara called her, but spoke of her as mother, and seemed to be handling the fact that she had two mothers with aplomb. It had taken time. And patience. Many a late night talk had helped Sara come to terms with things.

The girl's laughter filled the boutique.

'Do you think we could pretend we don't know them?' chuckled Angie. She saw pain flicker through Clare's eyes. 'I'm sorry, Sis. That was thoughtless.'

'Please, Angie. Don't apologise *again!* Otherwise I'll think you've stalled on number 8, or whichever step it is. Let's leave the past where it belongs.'

'Sure,' said Angie, reaching for Clare's hand and giving it a brief squeeze. 'You never regretted not having another child?'

'Frankly, no. Having a baby at sixteen was horrific. I wasn't prepared physically or emotionally. I've missed Sara, but that doesn't mean I wanted another child. I'm okay. Honestly.'

Angie smiled. How far they'd come. They each had different dramas and challenges, but at least they could be in the same room without one of them storming out.

Clare rested her head on Angie's shoulder as she had as a child. 'Where's Mum and Maggie?'

'They're wandering the shops 'at a more reasonable pace'. They both declared that a bridal frenzy was only for the young of the species. 'Not us,' they said. They'll meet 'the dizzy bridal party' for lunch in a quiet nook of *La Pizzaria*.'

'Mum seems to be doing better,' said Clare.

'Thanks to John and Maggie. I feel so bad.'

'Stop. You're doing it again. Don't forget one of the

agency nurses resigned because Mum called the police to report she was being held against her will. You must have been at your wit's end. There is some dementia, Angie. Don't be in denial about that.'

'I know. I'm just glad she's coping in her own home again. It's been a wild roller coaster these past few years.' Angie looked Clare directly in the eyes. 'How are you, Clare? Really. I hear you're doing some design work with Dave. How's that going?'

Clare's eyes misted. Angie had been so caught up in the drama of her own life that Clare often felt invisible. It was marvellous to have a growing friendship with her sister. She'd long given up on that. They'd avoided becoming involved in each other's struggles for fear of seeing their own agony mirrored there. Knowing that made it easier to forgive.

'We don't see each other much, but it's comfortable. It's as if I don't know the man he is now. It was so long ago. We collaborate on designs. He's very happy with Melanie. She's heavily pregnant—hoping not to go into labour during the service. I told her in our family that was the least she should worry about.'

'How true!' laughed Angie. 'I'm glad she'll be there, she's a real sweetie.'

They both fell silent, each in their own reverie.

'How are things with James?' asked Clare.

'So so. It'll take time. We speak occasionally.'

'Well, that's progress.' Clare soaked in the pleasure of watching the three girls try on dresses, do each other's hair while chatting nonstop about their style opinions. Sara executed a perfect pirouette and Clare's heart constricted. Her daughter had elegance and grace, but more importantly she'd come out of the last two years with joy and serenity.

Angie enjoyed the same scene with different emotions. How nearly she'd come to losing it all.

She'd been sober for 18 months.

At the time she thought there would never be an end to the anxiety, endless nights and buckets of tears. She remembered sitting in the grounds of the Fenmore Clinic, with the gentle breeze on her skin, feeling more alive, but also more terrified than she'd ever been. Just getting through the day was a huge hurdle back then. Her skin had crawled, her head was fuzzy and she sweated and paced through many lonely nights.

Never in her wildest dreams had she imagined she would come out of it all with a career. However, along with a bright young thing Dave had recommended, she was running the Chatswood branch. Sensibly downsized of course. She hadn't seen the need for a showroom and sold the allotment to a prestige car firm, then printed glossy brochures showcasing the limousines in exotic locations. The satisfaction she received in running the business surprised everyone. Finding she was a natural made Angie feel she had reclaimed the positives from her past. She'd just started night classes in business studies.

Looking back, she remembered thinking she would never survive the end of her marriage. But only six months after they separated, and the numbing weariness lifted, she realised she was relieved. Not only to be done with the charade, but leaving the pressure of her former lifestyle behind. Coming undone had terrified her more than she could say.

Surrendering to the life that was possible, instead of the life she thought she wanted was a key part of her progress. There was no going back. Not to that dark place. She looked at the glow on Clare's face and knew she and Clare shared a deep gratitude.

The girls muffled giggles. Ellie had wound a sash too tight. Lucy was gasping and Sara was holding her sides, shaking with laughter. 'No sashes, *please!*'

Lunch was a noisy affair. It would have been worse, but Iris laid down the law as soon as the girls trouped in. 'Mobiles off, girls, or you won't receive an invite to my 70th Birthday Bash.

'We didn't know about a birthday party,' said Sara.

'I said 'bash', darling. There's a difference,' said Iris, her eyes twinkling.

'I don't want to know,' said Lucy.

'Now there's a first,' said Maggie, laughing.

'I'm learning. Where's a menu? I'm starving. This bridal frenzy is exhausting.'

'You're loving it,' said Sara, grabbing Lucy around the neck as an excuse to steal her menu.

'Hey! Come on Sara. Share at least.'

'Of course, darling. Now that you have perfect sight you should be able to read it from there.'

'Not when I can only see the back!'

'I'm ready to order,' said Clare.

Ellie's phone vibrated on the table and Iris quickly picked it up and held it over the water jug until Ellie turned it off with a sigh. 'Your fella can do without you for half a day, Ellie.'

'Hmm. Maybe, but if we're late for Amanda again she won't let us have the boys for the weekend. Or she'll bring them late and mess us around. She's still hell bent on revenge—can't face that the marriage is over. Ben has his heart set on having the boys. If we put a foot wrong...'

Iris favoured Ellie with a hard stare.

'He's getting a divorce. Don't say anything, Nan.'

'Wouldn't dream of it.'

'How was Rome?' Angie asked Lucy.

It was time to change the subject of her eldest daughter's relationship. When she'd heard that Ellie had dumped Brian for Ben it had tested her newfound peace. But her resolve to let her children live their own lives had proved unexpectedly freeing. She was responsible for herself now. The children were grown. It was time for them to make their own way, without judgement.

She remembered one of her favourite affirmations by Dr Jeff Mullan, 'Tell me what you want me to be...and before you even say the words, know that I cannot be it. I can only be myself. Let me tell you what I want you to be...and before I can even say the words, I realise you can only be yourself. And that is how it's meant to be'.

'Yes, Lucy, we all want to hear about your first overseas trip with Romeo,' said Ellie.

'Spill, Lucy,' laughed Sara.

'Ooh, it was wonderful. It was his first visit even though his father was from there. I would've teased him that he didn't know what he was talking about, but his fictitious stories were so funny and romantic I let him ramble on.'

'Did you go anywhere else?' asked Clare.

'We did a quick tour of the Greek Islands. I took some photos for Duncan. It was gorgeous there. But nothing compared to the sitting in the fountain in front of Villa

Medici on the Pincio at midnight. It was magic. And magic only happens a few times in a girl's life.' Lucy sighed.

'Hmm. There is something about fountains,' said Sara.

She'd been sitting at a fountain when she met Elliot. She was attending a week long course on glazing and resins. It was hard to keep her mind on class work.

During a break in class, Sara sat on the edge of one of the conference ground's fountains, dangling her feet in the cool water. Carefree and young for the first time in months. Instead of working on her colour chart she was doodling.

'I didn't think faeries were in the curriculum,' said a voice.

Sara looked up into the sharp blue eyes of a tall man. She hadn't seen him before.

'I didn't know you were in our class,' said Sara, annoyed at the intrusion.

'I'm not. I'm the guest lecturer you missed yesterday.'

'Sorry. Flattering of you to notice my absence.'

'Maybe I simply read the student list. It's not hard to notice an empty, rather cluttered desk.'

'Creative people are messy.'

'Who told you that nonsense? You really are a lost cause—truanting, scribbling. Show me,' he said, sitting next to her on the raised edge of the fountain facing the other way.

191

This gave him a unique position to look her in the eye. And look he did.

It unnerved her. She was far more accustomed to younger men who fussed over her—sweet and calm by nature, men found themselves wanting to please her.

'This is really very good, Sara. You should take the fantasy art class.'

'Trying to drum up more business?'

'No, I'm being genuine. That a new thing for you?'

'Lately it is.'

He laughed at her honesty. 'I'm Elliot Brentwood. I meant you should *teach* the class, not be a student.'

'Oh...*Oh!*' Sara sighed. 'I seem to be permanently stuck in misunderstanding mode. Sorry.'

'How refreshing.'

'It's a blooming nuisance. I'm becoming like my sister, Lucy. It's very humbling—after years of picking on her for foot and mouth disease I'm outstripping her in leaps and bounds.'

'Under a lot of stress?'

'You don't know the half,' said Lucy.

'Sounds daunting,' said Elliot.

The delicate young woman in front of him was looking at him quite naturally now. The guarded look was gone. He'd noticed her the past week, and overheard some of her short conversations. She was very talented, but he suspected she hadn't found her real passion with her artwork. However, looking at her elegant pencil strokes on the page, he realised Miss Sara Belmore had a deeply sensitive soul.

'I won't bore you with the story,' she said.

'I cannot fully express my gratitude for that,' he said, 'I am only a man, after all.'

Sara laughed, and in that moment, Elliot Brentwood saw his future.

Taffeta rustled, silk caressed as the girls fussed outside the church. Last minute water spray was misted on white roses. The tiny flower-girl pushed the pageboy so she could commandeer the centre of the carpet. His lip trembled. His mother took him aside, straightened his bow tie, while slipping a little red car into his pocket.

'Hold up, Sara! Your veil is caught on something in your hair,' said Ellie. I've never seen a more impatient bride. You're supposed to be nervous.'

'I've never been more sure of anything, or anyone. Elliot is my rock,' said Sara, turning to Lucy. 'Why are you wearing that ring on your left hand, Lucy?'

'Oh that. Jamie and I were married in Rome.'

'Lucy!'

'What?'

Give me an ugly truth,
rather than a beautifully crafted lie.
For if your lie becomes my truth
then I am lost.

What can I find in life
if you deny me this?
That crafted miscreation
becomes the ugly thing.

Sooner, or later every lie slips,
unfurling chaos.
Like silk floating softly down,
then rending, tearing.

I can stand by your truth
no matter what.
But what can I do? Where can I be
with a broken lie?

I can build, and I can change,
anything.
If only, you give me
truth.

The Unprize

'Oh wow! The world just exploded in a riot of colour and...What?' Chelsea screamed into the phone. 'I'm at the Harbour Bridge and a million tonnes of fireworks just went off. I can't hear you, but that's probably because I'm *now deaf!*'

It was New Year's Eve. The noisy countdown to the New Year had just finished and the annual fireworks display had begun, lighting up the indigo sky. Chelsea was at the Opera House with a camera crew. There was a lull between the fireworks, then chuckling. Chelsea moaned as she realised her voice had carried to the film and stage crew.

'You did it again, didn't you!' screeched Leisa. She found Chelsea's antics endlessly entertaining.

'Did what?'

'Put your foot in it, didn't you? I wish I was there to see the looks on everyone's faces.' Leisa snorted.

That was the trouble with best friends; they knew you too well, thought Chelsea. 'What are you doing anyway?' she asked, ignoring the guffaws of the crew. 'You're supposed to be in labour. Hasn't my godchild arrived yet? You'd better get a move on. I am not going to fill in for you forever you know, this is your job I am slaving over down here.' Chelsea changed the mobile phone to her other ear as she struggled to catch Leisa's words. Leisa was gabbling on about some competition. 'Are you okay?' Chelsea asked in the next lull, her voice softening. The fireworks started again. Chelsea couldn't hear Leisa.

The colourful New Year's celebrations were the backdrop for a promotional photo shoot for Leisa's catering business. One of the models was sick and Chelsea filled in at the last minute. She consoled herself that with any luck would be unrecognizable with the dramatic makeup and the shoulder length Cleopatra style wig.

'*Another* competition,' moaned Chelsea.

Leisa had become a competition junkie since becoming pregnant. This time she'd entered the 'Daydream about Soap' competition. Chelsea had dictated some over-the-top nonsense to Leisa that was intended to satirise the show. The winner would be announced after the fireworks. Chelsea hated the soap with a vengeance. Overacted and deliberately schmaltzy, it was her idea of torture. She couldn't remember a word she'd dictated to Leisa. She'd leave as soon as the winner was announced.

She didn't notice a man who had watched her all evening from the comfort of a faded deck chair. The tall, dark man was sitting just behind the glare of the lights. Jack Devon narrowed his eyes to follow the movements of the woman who had entertained him on this long night where he had expected to face terminal boredom. From the minute she stepped out with her micro mini skirt under that ridiculously large apron and that sassy smile on her face he was enchanted. She tripped over the wires, she swore softly when she'd been unable to light the candle for the fondue. She dropped her glasses after putting them on and off to read the cue card. She'd gabbed all through her segment of the photo shoot to the riotous enjoyment of the crew. Jack guessed she had no concept of 'still' photography, or still anything for that matter. She was a refreshing delight, more delectable than the menu. Her constant chattering compared to the sultry silence of the others had been unashamedly hilarious. He loved a woman who didn't take herself too seriously.

The other models had vamped it up on cue, but Chelsea arrived with her silky black Cleopatra style wig askew and an apron ten times the size of the other girls. She was nervous initially, but when the candle wouldn't light she purred, 'Cooking up a storm in the bedroom takes a bit longer when the fire has gone out.' She leant in a mock seductive pose on the red satin sheets with a rose between her teeth and slipped off the bed, falling with her legs inelegantly in the air.

Jack had been doubled over with tears streaming down his eyes. He suspected the green eyed minx couldn't see the reaction of the crew and doubted she knew that the whole segment had been filmed by the news crew that was roaming the Quay.

A low rumbling sound combined with a tightening of her stomach made Chelsea realise that she was starving. Food, she thought, find food; now! Then she remembered a salad platter had been laid out for the models near their dressing tent. She giggled. It would have to be the safest place to keep food.

She tripped over the long legs of a man sitting inside the dressing tent. The models had left. Jack had moved from the boardwalk to get some peace from the noisy crowd. His face was shadowed. Without glancing in the direction of 'the feet' she muttered a vague apology. She quickly assessed him as one of the bored executives who managed to get through the endless obligatory year-end social events with a mixture of cocaine and booze. He hadn't even moved. Served him right. Dismissing all thought of him she found the food table. Her heart sank to her now-cramped stomach as she saw how little food was left.

Jack's mouth twitched in sheer enjoyment as he watched Chelsea circling the food table; her expressive eyes full of disappointment.

'I'd kill for a sandwich,' she said. 'This is do-able.' She lay several lettuce leaves down, then added crackers, dip, cheese, pesto, cherry tomatoes and rolled it into something resembling a wrap.

'What do you call that?' asked one of the crew.

'Groucho would know,' she responded; eyes twinkling. She wagged the wrap like a cigar, in a flawless caricature of the famous Marx brother.

'You're a scream, Cleopatra.'

Her appetite sated, Chelsea realised it was time to clean up. The models had thrown their plastic glasses on the Opera House steps. Honestly, would it kill them to bend down to pick up a few glasses! Apparently they could spend hours on the treadmill burning calories, but couldn't be bothered moving a muscle to save work for someone else.

Before adding the garbage bag to the growing pile of rubbish Chelsea tore the wig from her head to reveal a lush head of caramel curls.

He'd have to try and wangle an introduction. Relaxing back, he stretched his long legs now thoroughly cramped by the canvas deck chair. There was a crack as he hit the pavement, the timber frame of the chair in ludicrous pieces beneath him.

Chelsea heard the noise and looked up to see lanky limbs everywhere. Probably some drunken reveller. She wandered over to help. By the time she arrived Jack was on his feet massaging a bruised elbow that had connected with the hard cement.

Seizing the opportunity he held out a hand and said, 'Devon, I'm...Ja'

'Devon? Are you still talking to your mother after being named after a ham sandwich?' she queried, dropping his arm. 'You'll live, no blood loss.'

'Never mind … I...' Jack began, but one of the other catering staff had called out to Chelsea and she was gone. He didn't even know her name.

It obviously wasn't Cleopatra.

Author

Linda was born and raised in a small country town on the east coast of Australia, near Lake Macquarie. She gained the attention of a publisher when her short stories found critical acclaim on the ABC website, 'The Making of Modern Australia' and *A Curious & Inelegant Childhood* was published as *An Australian Childhood.*

Linda's short stories have been published in numerous anthologies: Coastlines 5 & 6 (Southern Cross University), Wood, Bricks & Stone (Catchfire Press) and Grieve (Hunter Writer's Centre) and Longing for Solitude (Stringybark Press). She has won creative writing awards, including first prize for The Legacy University Level Creative Writing Award and first prize for the Gabe Reynaud Creative Writing Award, and the Mater Misericordiae Grieve Writing Award. Linda's books feature her skill as an artist and illustrator.

Linda still writes and now lives in Adelaide where she operates an online business *LRB Publishing Services* that assists authors with design and formatting.

Other titles by Linda

Nonfiction:

I'm not broken, I'm just different (Asperger's Syndrome)
An Australian Childhood

Poetry:

Verse

Adult fiction:

Behind Whispering Hands
Scarlett doesn't live here anymore
The Unprize
A broken hallelujah
Under the Bracken Fern

Children's books:

A Tabby Never Forgets
An Angels Tears
Callan the Chameleon (Asperger's Syndrome)
Dusty Bunny's Very Important Job
Ethereal Land
Izzy & Pudding the Cat
I want a monkey!
Madam Iris Bigglesworth
The Frog that Hiccupped
When the stars move
Who Stole Christmas?

Publisher of the anthologies:

We are Australian'
The Great Australian Shed
Waltzing Matilda